Praise for David W. B

A writer with an enormous sense of humar
San Francisco Review of Books

Berner writes with vulnerability, humor, and grace.
Chicago's *This Much Is True*

Berner's writing captures the raw and real essence of what it is
to be human.
KDKA Radio

Walks with Sam

The poet Wallace Stevens wrote that sometimes the answer
comes with a walk around the lake. In my case, it's a daily walk
around the neighborhood at dawn with the dogs that provides
an answer to the unknown challenges of the day. Writer
David W. Berner knows this truth better than most, a timeless
phenomenon splendidly explored and revealed in his wise and
insightful *Walks with Sam*, a moving memoir about how a young
dog can teach an old man new tricks about mindfulness and
presence. Hard to remember when I've enjoyed a walk with two
friends more, a reminder of the important things dogs help us
discern about ourselves, and the world around us.
James Dodson, author of *Faithful Travelers* and *Final Rounds*

Through Berner's adoring relationship with Sam, the reader
realizes that though humans and their canine companions are
different, the love they share for each other undeniably bridges
this gap. This is a highly recommended and heartwarming read.
Well written, immensely satisfying, and thought provoking.
International Review of Books

An inherently fascinating and unfailingly thoughtful read from beginning to end.
Midwest Book Review

October Song

October Song strikes all the right chords; the high notes and the low notes of a life's journey—the losses, the lessons, the loves. Composed with tenderness and affection, Berner's heartfelt and ultimately life-affirming joy ride teaches us that you're never too old to roll down the window, crank it up and belt it out.
Randy Richardson, author of *Lost in the Ivy*

Berner succeeds, once again, as a master storyteller. Music can tell the story of our past. Lyrics evoke memories; melodies make the heart thump like it did on a first date. *October Song* brings the reader through a mix tape of life and tells his tale of new love while traveling through landscapes and time. Each chapter reads like a beloved song.
Geralyn Hesslau Magrady, author of *Lines*

October Song is a beautifully authentic memoir that reminds us there are no limits on dreams, creativity is boundless, and nothing in life is finite when we let go of our self-imposed rules.
Windy City Reviews

Sandman

a golf tale

Sandman

a golf tale

David W. Berner

ROUNDFIRE
BOOKS

Winchester, UK
Washington, USA

JOHN HUNT PUBLISHING

First published by Roundfire Books, 2022
Roundfire Books is an imprint of John Hunt Publishing Ltd., No. 3 East St., Alresford,
Hampshire SO24 9EE, UK
office@jhpbooks.com
www.johnhuntpublishing.com
www.roundfire-books.com

For distributor details and how to order please visit the 'Ordering' section on our website.

Text copyright: David W. Berner 2021

ISBN: 978 1 78904 912 1
978 1 78904 913 8 (ebook)
Library of Congress Control Number: 2021932919

Design: Stuart Davies

UK: Printed and bound by CPI Group (UK) Ltd, Croydon, CR0 4YY
Printed in North America by CPI GPS partners

We operate a distinctive and ethical publishing philosophy in
all areas of our business, from our global network of authors to
production and worldwide distribution.

Also by David W. Berner

Walks with Sam
October Song
A Well-Respected Man
Things Behind the Sun

For my father, Norman F. Berner

I think, that if I touched the earth,
It would crumble;
It is so sad and beautiful,
So tremulously like a dream.
Dylan Thomas

Sandman

Most everyone called him Jimmy. A few called him Jack. There were those at Old Elm who were unsure if either was his real name, but he answered to both, nonetheless. The talk had been that he grew up somewhere nearby, but like this name, this was uncertain. And if someone did know for sure, they didn't say. Most players would call out or tip their hats as they walked up the fairway and the short hill toward the 5th green. Jimmy, in his soiled Top Flite ball cap would wave and smile, craggy and crooked. He was always there, it seemed, sitting on his coat near the maple at the property fence a few yards west of the green, encouraging a putt to fall or clapping for a good chip shot. But it had been several days now, and no one had seen Jimmy.

"He must be on a bender," the young boy said, propping his stand bag on the fringe off the left side of the green. "He kind of disappeared."

His friend, another boy about the same age, shrugged his shoulders.

"We've been doing this for two summers now, you and me, playing almost every day and every time we see that guy," the first boy said.

"I heard he sleeps in that sand trap," said the second boy, pointing to the green's only bunker. "Like a goat or sheep or something."

"I think they'd throw him out if he really did that."

"Probably smells like my uncle," the second boy continued, recalling the time his approach shot landed close to Jimmy's usual spot.

"Your uncle?"

"Like shit. Booze, probably," he said, stroking his putt to gimme range.

The first boy's shot had landed on the green's apron. He used his putter to knock the ball a few inches beyond the cup.

"Pick it up," his friend said.

"Remember that time he pretended to be an announcer,

3

doing play-by-play like the guys on TV?" the first boy asked.

"Here we are at Augusta," the second boy whispered in a golf voice. "Yep. It was funny. I think you made that putt and he cheered like somebody in the gallery on the tour."

As the boys threw their golf bags on their shoulders and headed for the 6th tee, the first boy wondered aloud, "Maybe he died or something."

Jimmy was thin and gaunt, his shoulders slumped into his bony build, his hands spotted from the sun, his temples held deep wrinkles, his voice full of tobacco smoke. If a golfer got close enough, he could see his yellow teeth, his salt-and-pepper stubble, and the red, blotchy skin of his cheeks. His eyes, however, deep brown like coffee beans, always appeared clear and alert, and around his neck he wore a small silver cross that glistened when the sun hit it at a particular angle. One might bet he never took it off.

After the round, the boys bought sodas at the counter in the clubhouse snack bar and took them to the picnic table on the small patio overlooking the 18th green. The first group from the old timer's league was putting out.

"That was for an 8. You can bet on that," the first boy said to his friend as the last putt dropped and the man with a belly like a basketball and a black compression brace around his right knee pumped his fist.

The second boy laughed. "It was really a 10, though. I don't think they take any more than an 8 on the card. Make their own rules."

"I saw one of the guys take out a carpenter's measuring tape from his bag once to measure his buddy's ball from the pin," said the first boy. "Laid it right out on the green."

"Some closest-to-the-pin bet, probably."

The big belly man noticed the boys watching and said, "You see that putt, fellas? That was for the money."

"Nice," the first boy said.

"It's my recent good luck. Had it for two weeks, now," the man said, removing his ball from the hole with the tiny suction cup at the end of his putter grip.

"Got to take advantage when you can," the first boy added.

"Ever since Jimmy blessed me, I've been a different player."

The boys looked at one another. "The homeless dude?" the second boy whispered. The first boy shrugged.

"Do you mean the guy that always hangs round the 5th green?" the first boy asked the man.

"Yep. He saw me four-putt one day," the man said, walking to his cart. "Said he had a cure. Stood up and did this crazy dance and chanted something weird. Said it would remove the bad spirits from my bag. He was trying to make me feel better, make me laugh. But guess what? Ever since, I'm making absolutely everything."

"Guy must know something," the second boy said, smiling.

The old man stood near the edge of the green at the cart path, shaking hands with his buddies, and turned back to the boys, "Hey, by the way, did you see him out there today?"

"Nope. Wasn't there," the first boy said.

* * *

The boys finished their sodas and stood together with their bags at their sides at the turnaround outside the main clubhouse door, waiting for their ride. Old Elm Golf Course was a public place with a simple old-school layout and not a single elm tree. The brick clubhouse had a small pro shop and a five-table grill. Nancy, the woman who ran the food counter was known for making a tasty tuna salad sandwich. The 9-hole lady's league played on Tuesday mornings in the summer. The 18-hole men's league, mostly a bunch of old guys, played a couple of times a week. The boys got out for a few dollars as juniors. The course was built in the 1920s, but underwent some renovations in the

'80s, mostly the traps. The fairways were bluegrass and the greens bent. They would have been in better shape if more people replaced their divots and fixed their ball marks. But it was a solid, fair, and pretty track, no homes around it, the land moving along nicely up and down a few hills and through strands of big oaks. The boys tried to play at least twice a week when school was out. The second boy's mother had dropped them there in the early morning that day, and he had called her for a lift home.

"How long? Did she say?" the first boy asked.

"Not sure," the second boy said, his head scrolling through his phone.

From the west side of the clubhouse, the boys heard the chug of a golf cart and a sharp high-pitched bark. The head greenskeeper was making his rounds with his dog, a wiry short-haired terrier mutt that never stopped moving, jumping, or running loops around the cart as the greenskeeper drove the course. Even when the dog was in the golf cart, it spun in the seat and stood upright with its front paws on the top of the seat's back cushion to get a better look at the scenery, as if guarding something.

"Hey, young men," the greenskeeper said, bringing his cart to a stop in front of them. "How'd it go out there?"

Both mumbled something, avoiding eye contact.

"Beautiful day," the greenskeeper said, surveying the sky. "A fuckin' birdie of a day, don't ya think?" The greenskeeper had been at Old Elm as long as anyone could remember. He started at the course as a young man out of college, cutting grass. The boys were always laughing about how he probably has never allowed three minutes to pass without saying fuck.

"Hey, you gents didn't see that fuckin' bum out there today, did ya?" The greenskeeper's admiration of the day had quickly turned to matters of course maintenance.

"Wasn't there," the first boy said.

"Better fuckin' not be. I had to chase him off the course a few days ago. Right before sunrise, we found the fucker walking the 5th fairway in his fuckin' bare feet. I heard he did that. This time I caught him. Strolling along. And then last week, one of my workers out raking traps in the morning found him sleeping in a fuckin' bunker. I called the cops on him."

The boys looked at each other. *So, it's true,* they both thought. *He sleeps in the sand trap.*

"Can't do anything to him if he's hanging around on the other side of the fuckin' fence, but if he comes on my course. Well, fuck him."

The boys nodded.

"Anyway," he said, the dog now back in the cart after a lap around it. "Carry on. See you soon out there. Hit 'em straight and replace your fuckin' divots!"

The boys watched the cart turn the corner near the bag stand and move across the 9th fairway.

"Yeah, fucker," the second boy said to the first, punching his friend on the shoulder. "Replace your fuckin' divots!"

The boys laughed.

Fifteen minutes passed and no ride. The second boy's mother had texted that she was held up at the grocery store.

"I think I'll stick around some," the first boy said, breaking the few minutes of silence that had passed. "Maybe hit some balls."

"Yeah, whatever," the second boy said.

"I can call my mom later for a ride."

They agreed to play again in two days and the first boy headed for the range.

* * *

The 5th hole at Old Elm may not be the prettiest, but the fairway runs along a gentle hill and swoops through a grove of massive trees. If there weren't other holes on the course with postcard views, the 5th would be right up there. The putting surface is also near a wooden fence and about 25 yards from the road, sapping its chances of being the course's most beautiful hole. But its position makes it just right for Jimmy, a good spot for watching players and a simple climb over the fence to the course.

Even when it was chilly or there was drizzle, Jimmy was at the 5th at sunrise, if he hadn't spent the night there. He shook out his old brown coat on the grass and sat quietly for a few minutes to listen to the early birds, the chirps and tweets that signal the kind of day that was coming. The louder the birds, the more beautiful the day, Jimmy believed. He would take off his boots with the thin soles and the mismatched laces, slip off his dirty white tube socks, and wiggle his toes. The fence was low enough to navigate barefooted, and even in July, the grass was cool to his touch, especially the long rough. Jimmy welcomed this. Feeling that chill reminded him he was alive.

This is how it would go when Jimmy was on the course. At the green's edge, facing the tee box some 390 yards away, Jimmy took deep breaths, closed his eyes, and began to walk down the middle of the fairway. He was blind to the world, but it didn't matter in the early hour. The sunlight hadn't yet cracked the horizon. With each slow step, he allowed all of his senses to take over. The birds chirped, there was the mustiness of dirt and dampness of dewy grass, and the turf gave in like a pillow each time his toes pushed off for the next stride.

After about 75 yards, Jimmy would open his eyes, and stand in the center of the fairway, slowly turn his body 360 degrees, his head angled slightly upward to survey the sky and the tops of the trees. Faint morning light would begin to permit shadows. Some mornings he saw the silhouette of the hawk that nested in the tallest tree about 150 yards down the fairway. He loved to watch it soar when it was feeding, admiring its grace as it would dive to tear its talons into an unsuspecting rabbit. The great bird was not a beast, Jimmy believed, but rather a majestic creature doing what Mother Nature designed. Jimmy had cried watching that hawk, knowing it was bringing food to its nest for its partner, its mate for life, the one with which it worked together to nourish its babies in the spring.

At the tee box, Jimmy knelt to run his fingers through the manicured grass, soft like the fur of a kitten. He put his nose to it and breathed in, the scent of earth filling his lungs. He again closed his eyes and listened. By now, the sound of the birds had changed. They were less excited, and the songs less intense. The day was beginning, and the birds' work was underway, darting along the land in search of worms and grubs, the hunt to stay alive. And for Jimmy, it was much the same, his own kind of hunt, another day to embrace in whatever way his worn-down body and mind would allow. He had accepted this life a long time ago, a life with nowhere to be and nowhere to go. Some days were harder than others; Jimmy would admit this to himself. And so, on those days, after he had walked the fairway and back to the green, before the sun was fully up and the work crews and dewsweepers were still an hour away, Jimmy pulled his hat down over his eyes, curled in his legs, and burrowed himself into the greenside bunker, up against the trap's high side like the ancient sheep at St. Andrews, and tried to capture a dream.

* * *

The boy had a handful of coins, a bunch of quarters and dimes that he had used as ball markers were found at the bottom of his bag, enough money to afford a small bucket of forty balls. His father, who had taught him the game, had always thought it best to start with the wedge and work your way up the clubs to the driver, hitting five balls each. After this, one should simulate a hole. Start with the driver, three-wood, a hybrid, a short iron, then produce a chip shot with the most lofted club, hitting only one ball with each as if you were making your way down the fairway.

"Still got that buttery swing, young man," said the ranger from his cart along the path.

The ranger was a retired engineer who in his younger days played on a mini tour or two, and still regularly scored in the mid 80s. He was at the course three days a week, each day wearing his signature white bucket hat, crisp and clean with the red headband and the Old Elm logo in the middle — an oversized golf ball under the canopy of a big tree. He accepted the ranger job a few years ago for free golf and to give him something to do. His daughter had moved to the next state several hundred miles away, his wife gone ten years now.

The boy struck his 6-iron, the sharp snap of metal on ball sweet and true. He and the ranger watched the ball rise and fall with a sight draw and settle next to a yellow flag 170 yards out.

"Pure," the ranger said.

"Thanks. Wish I could hit it like that all the time," the boy said.

The boy picked up his wedge, aimed at the red flag 65 yards away, and made a smooth half-swing from an open stance. The ball came to rest two feet from the bottom of the stick.

"So sweet," the ranger said from his seat in the cart. "Golf team in high school?"

"Hmm, yeah, I guess," the boy said, pulling a white tee from his pocket, a ball from the overturned bucket, and setting up for his driver.

"You *guess*?" The ranger couldn't imagine the boy hesitating. He was a natural, he thought. *Talent like that shouldn't be wasted.*

The boy launched the ball 230 yards, nearly to the far end of the range.

"My dad says the same thing," the boy said, watching as the

ball came to rest. "You sound like him."

"You ought to listen to your dad, son."

The boy reached for his 3-wood. "I have to work more on my putting if I'm going to do the golf team thing."

For the next few minutes, the ranger watched in silence as the boy struck balls, one after another, each leaving the clubface with a crack, ascending like a rocket, descending like a butterfly about to light on a blade of grass.

The walkie-talkie crackled. There was a foursome, the same group that every week slowed things down at the tough par-3 over water, dropping three and four balls into the drink.

"I gotta get to work," the ranger said. "Don't know how they can keep losing all those balls every single time."

"Hey, before you leave," the boy said, "do you know anything about that guy that hangs around 5?"

"Jack, yeah, Jimmy, or whatever. He's always there."

"Not today. Not the last couple, either, I heard."

"Well, he'll be there tomorrow, I'm sure. It's the guy's job, right?" The ranger turned his cart toward the path that leads to the back nine and stopped again for a moment. "You know he used to caddie in Scotland?"

"He was a caddie? For the pros?"

"No, just a regular caddie on some of the courses there when he was a young guy. Heard that somewhere. It was many years ago. Think it's true, though," the ranger said. "He might have caddied at the Old Course."

The boy's father wanted his son to take the caddie test at the country club this summer. But the boy wasn't keen on it. He wondered about that now.

* * *

No one had ever seen it, but there had been talk once amongst a foursome of regulars sitting around a table in the grill that

Jimmy kept a photograph in the front pocket of his jeans. One golfer claimed Jimmy had told him about it—an off-handed comment when the golfer had joked after making a long putt on the 5th that he wanted a picture of the ball falling in the hole, a way to capture the moment. He had made par, a rarity, and he wanted evidence. "Photos tell the real story," Jimmy had said, smiling after congratulating the golfer, and using his hands to pretend to click a camera. "I've had one for a lot of years. Reminds me so I don't forget things." An off-color Polaroid, Jimmy had said, one with three of the corners bent and one torn, crumpled from being tucked inside his faded Wranglers. The golfer wondered but didn't ask. But after the foursome finished the hole and began to walk toward the cart path at the back of the green, Jimmy said, "It's an old friend. Don't look at it all that much. But I know it's there. I always know it's there." One of the golfers teased Jimmy about what he thought must have been an old high school crush. Jimmy gave a throaty laugh.

She was a redhead, freckles around the edges of her nose and the corners of her blue eyes. In the photo she wears jeans and a blue top and leans against a short stone fence on a hill overlooking a treeless field. She is squinting into the sun, smiling. An errant strand of hair covers a cheek, blown there by a breeze.

It was in St. Andrews that he met her. She was working tables at The Jigger Inn not far from the 17th green of the Old Course. One chilly night, as she tossed logs on the open-hearth fireplace, struggling a bit to stoke the embers to life, Jimmy stepped in. An old Boy Scout, he told her. Jimmy rearranged the logs and blew on the glowing wood, and after most everyone had gone for the night, and there was little for her to do, he and the girl sat by that fire, sharing drams of Monkey Shoulder. She was a student at St. Andrews University, grew up in Ireland— Ballyhack, County Wexford—and stayed in Scotland to work between semesters. Jimmy had come to caddie. College was over but he wasn't ready to find what he called a real job, he had joked. He liked the idea of being his own man, a maverick on a beautiful piece of Scotland's coast. The girl had not met anyone before like Jimmy, no one with his spirit, she believed. They were both too young to become their parents, she had told him, agreeing, at least at the time, with his lifestyle. That summer they spent many days together. He visited her family in Ballyhack. The photo was taken with her father's old camera on a bright afternoon on a drive through the country somewhere near the ruins of Ferns Castle. That was many years ago.

* * *

The boy tossed three balls to the green, and using the head of his putter, he lined them up—the first at his feet, the second five inches from the first, and the third the farthest away. With his feet spread equidistant, his left arm by his side and palm against his thigh, the boy used his right hand to rest the head of the blade putter, his father's old Wilson 8802 on the green's surface behind the nearest ball, the ball's equator at the center in front of the clubface. The boy tilted his head forward, his eyes on an imaginary straight line down to the putter. He turned to the left and glanced toward the cup, some six feet away, then back to the ball, joined his left hand together with his right on the worn leather grip, looked again to the cup and back to the ball one last time. In a slow, deliberate motion with his eyes locked on the Titleist logo, the boy brought the putter head back a few inches behind the ball, and with the action of a pendulum, executed a smooth stroke. Without looking, the boy heard a muted clunk and mild rattle, the sound of the ball falling against the bottom of the cup. He stepped forward to the second ball, and again with eyes away from the hole, the boy made the same silky stroke. Again, a clunk and rattle. But on the third, despite finding a yoga-like rhythm, the boy did not hear the ball strike the plastic cup. When he lifted his eyes, the ball had stopped right of the hole, a half-an-inch offline.

"You're not gonna let that happen again, are you?"

The question came from over the boy's shoulder. One of the old guys who played most every day was pulling his putter from his cart. The boy recognized the man to say hello but didn't know his name.

"Two out of three in baseball is pretty good," the boy said. "But yeah, I like to make them all."

"This is not baseball," the old man said. "Gotta bring the course to its knees."

The boy laughed. "Probably not going to do that."

"What do you mean?" the old man asked. "That's what *I'm* trying to do. Have to. Otherwise, I'm playing with my dick out here."

The old man dropped a single ball to the green and tapped a long putt, about 15 feet away, toward the cup on the far side of the practice putting surface. It rolled over a small rise, fell hard to the left then back to the right, and came to rest about two feet from the hole on the left side.

"That's a good lag," the boy said.

"Ah shit," the old man grumbled. "I have to make that. Gotta make that."

"Still pretty decent."

"Ever read *Harvey Penick's Little Red Book*? The one that came out a few years ago?" the old man asked. "You're probably too young. But Harvey says to take dead aim. Wants you to believe you can make everything. That's how I go about this game."

The boy thought of what his father once told him: *If you expect miracles in golf, you're going to be disappointed.*

The old man reached in his pocket for a second ball, dropped it to the green, and took his stroke. The ball rolled and tumbled and missed the hole again. "God dammit," the old man muttered. He stood silent, staring at the hole. "Makes me want to throw the putter in the lake."

"What do they say about golf being relaxing?" the boy wondered.

"I've always played this way. Kind of hotheaded, you know. Ever get like that?"

"Throwing clubs? No."

"I flung an old putter of mine over the fence in the big, gnarly mess of tall prairie grass and weeds off the 5th green once. Simply launched it."

The boy was silent.

"That homeless guy that hangs out there, Jack or something, tried to calm me down and went looking for it. I told him, forget it. Fuck it."

"Did he find it?" the boy asked.

"He was still looking when I headed for the 6th."

"Too thick in there, huh?"

"Funny thing," the old man said. "I'm playing the next day, walking up to the 5th green, and there he is, sitting in his spot as usual, smiling, and in his hand is my piece-of-shit putter. He's waving it in the air. Got a present for you, I think he said."

"So, he found it?"

"Yeah. I told him to keep it, though. Goddamn club. He must have looked for a good while. I'm sure he sold it to somebody."

"Kind of nice of him," the boy said, "to find it, I mean, and hold onto it for you."

"He probably thought I'd have a reward for him or something. You know how that goes."

Jimmy had seen his share of angry golfers while spending his days along the 5th hole, guys whipping their clubs into the air after failing for the third time to get out of the greenside bunker. One man pounded his club into the ground after stubbing a chip, leaving a deep slice in the green's apron. Another kicked his golf cart so hard his shoe flew off. A lot of "fucks" and "son-of-a-bitches." One of the most creative expletives came from a cigar chomping fat guy in one of the Thursday afternoon foursomes who watched as his ball rimmed the hole and ended up six inches to the right. "You motherfucking, ass-eating, dick-sucking, dirty, filthy, crab-infested whore!"

"Come on, now," Jimmy had said to the angry man, "It's a beautiful day. And besides, there's always another hole, another shot, another walk to make."

When he caddied at St. Andrews, Jimmy carried the bags of amateur golfers of every kind of ability from around the world. And although many were over the moon about playing at golf's Mecca, Jimmy believed some were unrealistic about their level of skill or lack thereof, far too demanding of their below-average games, and relentless in the crazy pursuit of some unattainable excellence. There were the golfers who moaned about having to walk the course—no carts permitted—or complained about the notorious St. Andrews wind. There were the guys who blamed their caddies for a lousy club selection or bad advice on an approach shot, even as they were well aware that St. Andrews' caddies were the best anywhere. In Jimmy's first month of looping, there was the golfer who protested that he couldn't possibly play good golf on the fairways of the Old Course because the grass wasn't right somehow. "It's not normal. It's too tight," he groused to his caddie over the first several holes. Jimmy was carrying another's bag in the group when the unhappy golfer angrily confronted his caddie, a Scotsman who had been looping for more than twenty years. "What kind of grass is this anyway?" the golfer snapped as he marched down the 9th fairway after sending his second shot into the gorse on the left side of the green. The caddie stopped, looked the man directly in the eyes, and said, "It's fuckin' green grass. Now go find your fuckin' ball."

That's when the true meaning of the game began to emerge for Jimmy, again hearing the words of his father, his first teacher, the words said long ago when Jimmy was learning the game as a boy. "Take what the course gives you," he would say. It was an old golf adage, but a good one. The exchange between the surly golfer and his caddie triggered a memory and a deeper reality. The game was much more than what Jimmy had always thought it was supposed to be—a battle against the course or a war with Old Man Par, the never-ending challenge to score and win. Jimmy was uncovering the mystical truth behind the game. He was coming to believe that the game was not sport or competition, not about striking the ball as hard and as far as one could, and it was not about knocking the ball in the hole in the fewest possible strokes. Those were only vehicles for the journey. The meaning of golf was instead found in the land, in the sky, and in the slow steps of a long walk.

* * *

Nancy was surprised how much the boy liked her famous sandwich.

"What kid eats tuna salad?" she asked. "Your mother raised you right."

"Thanks, I guess so," the boy said, taking the plastic plate from the grill counter. The sandwich, made with toasted wheat bread, tomato, and raw onion was wrapped in butcher paper, a large dill pickle next to it.

"Then you go and put yellow mustard on it," Nancy said, "and that's a little strange, young man."

"My father does that, too. I guess I got it from him."

"Got some other things from him, too," Nancy said, winking at the boy. "I heard he plays a good game."

Whenever the boy was without enough money for a bite of food, Nancy spotted him. Today, after using up most of the change he had in his bag for the range, he was penniless for something to eat. The boy never missed paying his debt when he returned to the course. His mother gave him a $30 weekly allowance as long as he took the garbage to the curb on Monday nights, cut the lawn twice a week, and folded his own clean clothes from the laundry basket. It got him a couple of cheap junior rounds a week in the summer, and a few play-as-much-as-you-want deals with a few bucks remaining, sometimes.

"I guess I should've learned by now," the boy said. "Bring enough money if I'm gonna spend all day here and eat, too."

"It happens," Nancy said. "You're good for it."

It seems Nancy had always been behind the grill's counter at Old Elm. No one remembers anyone else working there. She moved a bit slow, but she was always smiling, joking with the regulars about the erasers on their golf pencils, and how they used them a bit too often.

"Am I the only one?" the boy asked.

"Who gets this super special deal?"

"Yeah. Are you nice to everybody?"

"Well, your buddy gets a break now and then," Nancy said, speaking of the other boy who had gone home. "A couple of the old timers get an extra pickle. But, no, you're the only one. You're it, young man. Special. Very special." Nancy offered a crooked grin and another wink.

"Ah, that's so bogus," the boy said.

Nancy had given a lot of people breaks over the years, and everyone, including her boss knew it. On hot summer days, she had slipped some iced tea to Jose and Marcus, the early-day grounds crew guys. She would see them from the window of the grill, sweating and wiping their brows as they dug and raked the four bunkers around the 9th green, the ones that forever washed out in a rainstorm. She would wink, they would wink back, and in minutes two iced teas would be sitting on the picnic table on the patio behind the 8th green.

"It's all in a day's work, you know?" Nancy said, wiping the countertop with a wet towel.

The boy stood at the counter, tearing open plastic packets

and squirting yellow mustard on the tuna. "Your secret's out," the boy said. "Not really a secret, you know?"

Nancy looked behind her, to the left and right, and leaned over the counter toward the boy, her index finger coaxing him closer.

"Got one true secret, though," she whispered.

The boy turned his ear to her.

"Jimmy," Nancy said.

The boy scrunched his forehead, uncertain if he had heard her correctly.

"Yep," Nancy continued. "I drop off a couple of water bottles, or some other drink or two, and some turkey slices, some bread, whatever I got that day. I go home that way, where the road turns near the 5th green. I pull over with food for him as often as I can."

"Really?"

"Probably some law against it, some restaurant thing or health department garbage. But I figure, why let it go to waste? It's perfectly good food. Let's give it away. Let's give it to Jimmy."

"You do this every day?" the boy asked.

"Pretty close."

"And you know him, you know Jimmy?"

"I know him like everyone else, I guess," Nancy said, turning away. "The nine-hole ladies ignore the guy. Act like he's the plague. I always say hello when my group comes through."

"That's nice."

"I know some Jimmys," she said. "I have always known my share of Jimmys."

Alone at the table closest to the door, the boy ate his sandwich. He texted his mother, asking to stay longer at the course and if that was all right with her. The boy was not ready to go home, not ready to leave. He didn't understand why, exactly, but for whatever reason, there was now a strong tug to stick around, to be at Old Elm for as long as he could, as if he might not get another chance, another day quite like this.

The boy took the last bite of pickle, tossed his napkin and plastic plate in the trash can at the door, and turned to Nancy as she straightened the salt and pepper shakers on the table near the hall that led to the pro shop.

"He wasn't there today," the boy said.

"Jimmy?" Nancy asked, knowing the answer. "Yeah, I heard that. Wasn't there yesterday either. Maybe the day before. That worries me."

"He's always there."

"They chased him off the course again, that I know. The greenskeeper doesn't like him much. Jimmy always come back, though."

"He walks the 5th fairway in the dark, right?"

"And sleeps in the bunker," Nancy whispered.

The boy smiled. "Thought that was only a rumor."

"He's the Sandman," Nancy said, her hands on her hips, her eyes twinkling. "Someone gave him that name a long time ago. The Sandman."

* * *

Some young travelers move around Europe with a light rail ticket and backpack. Some head off on a long American road trip. Rich kids are sent to Cancun for Spring Break. Years ago, it was the Peace Corps for many. For Jimmy, it was Scotland. He finished up his college undergrad years and set his sights on St. Andrews, and a summer of caddying and all those pubs, more than any other city in Scotland. Before real life started, it was Jimmy's plan to live differently. And although he revered the Old Course, it was the town that first captured him when he arrived, land meeting sea, golf merging with the townspeople, the community, everything about the town's existence woven into the ancient game. One can hardly tell where the Old Course ends and the town begins. In America, golf is fenced in. In St. Andrews, the most famous golf course in the world and those who live near it are linked, intertwined, beating with the same heart.

Before leaving home for overseas, Jimmy read as much as he could about the Old Course and all the other courses at St. Andrews, like the New Course, the toughest of them all. He learned that Americans don't understand what *old* truly is. The New Course was established in 1895; the Old can be traced as far back as the fifteenth century. When he first arrived, he did his time caddying at a course a bit south of St. Andrews. With his high school summers at the country club near where he grew up, he had enough knowledge for the caddie master at the Crail Golfing Society to take him on as a looper. He had his share of humiliation at his hometown country club. One member regularly ordered him to run back to the clubhouse in the middle of the outward nine to snatch a bag of pretzels and a Sprite. Jimmy found the players at Crail, and Scotsmen in general, more knowledgeable of the game and a lot less prickly. Arrogance was not mandatory as it was at America's private clubs. Jimmy spent a month at Crail but every few days he would arrive at St. Andrews, hoping to get the nod. In those days, it was easier to snatch a caddie position. St. Andrews insists on a long training period now. Then, if you passed a written test on etiquette and answered a few questions about course knowledge, and would promise to show up on time, you had a reasonable shot, if you also could get on the good side of the caddie master. He favored the locals, the old timers. This meant keeping your mouth shut and showing up in the morning as early as possible. And of course, if you didn't know the game it would eventually show, and you'd be gone.

For weeks, Jimmy got nothing, then one day he heard his name.

"Jimmy! You're up."

The caddie master didn't much like American kids, thought they were all knuckleheaded frat boys. But Jimmy knew his place, showed it, and on a drizzly late afternoon, Jimmy got his first Old Course loop, a twosome, a husband and wife on vacation from Milwaukee. They had saved for over a year to be there.

"It's a double," the caddie master moaned and zeroed in on Jimmy's eyes. "I'm watching you."

Jimmy believed he was ready. He knew not to walk on the left side of the fairway on the opening hole and block the group coming up the 18th. If another caddie saw him do that, he was dead. He knew a newcomer could easily mis-club the 11th green. If one of the veteran caddies saw that, Jimmy would be forever ridiculed, and certainly the caddie master would get word of it before the round was over. There was little room for error on these links, and if he fumbled, goofed up, goofed off, misjudged anyone, anything, or anywhere, he would never loop again.

The day went smoothly, he thought, and walking up 18, Jimmy offered to take a photo of the man and his wife with the camera they had brought along on the trip. The light rain had stopped, and the couple smiled for the photograph, standing together on the Swilcan Bridge. At the green after the putts were made, having no idea what their final scores had been and not caring to tally them, the husband and wife embraced, these two retired teachers had thought the day would never come, never believed they could have afforded the trip, never thought it would be possible to play at the home of golf.

Jimmy stood at the back of the final green witnessing the joy. This is the part of the game non-golfers don't understand, he thought. You have to play it to know it. You can't see it watching the pros on TV, and you can't read about it in *Golf Digest*. To the one who has never played, golf looks to be one thing, but it is really something else.

The tip was generous enough, but Jimmy wouldn't have cared if it had been pennies. He had completed his first loop at St. Andrews and was riding high. As he walked to the caddie station to turn in his bib, Jimmy could see the caddie master waiting, his arms crossed across his chest, a cigarette tight between his lips, his eyes locked on each step Jimmy took. What could he have done? Where did he mess up? What did he forget? Did he wrongly identify Hells Bunker? How could he have screwed that up? The Principal's Nose? Was that it? The photo on the 18th, did he hold up the group behind?

"Thank you, sir," Jimmy sighed, handing the bib to the caddie master. "This was a dream come true."

The silence seemed to last for much too long.

"Guess you're gonna live another fuckin' day," the caddie master growled.

From then on, Jimmy received regular work. Not every day at first, but in time, most days. And most nights Jimmy ended up at The Jigger Inn to see the red-haired girl, and to try to fit in with the loopers who sometimes hung out there when they had a few extra dollars and wanted to splurge. One might say, this is where Jimmy learned to drink. He had his share of beer in his school days, but he found out soon enough that no one drinks like a Scotsman, and no Scotsman drinks like a St. Andrews caddie.

* * *

In mid-afternoon, the boy took a seat on the hill behind the 18th at Old Elm, in front of the picnic table near the grill door to watch the golfers hit their approaches and drop their final putts. The hole was a short par-5, but few players hit the green in regulation. It was nearly always the fourth shot that finally made the putting surface. Most golfers at Old Elm, like most golfers everywhere, more often than not, underclubbed their shots to the green. Everyone insists they can hit it farther than they really can. The boy wondered if that fact wasn't far more about ourselves than about how golfers play the game. People believe they're thinner than they really are, have more hair than they really do, are smarter than their brains allow, stronger than their muscles will permit, and too many think they can hit an 8-iron 155 yards. There may be only a half-dozen regulars at Old Elm who can match that distance, the good players. But the brain, our spirit, and our fragile egos do not always allow us to see things as they truly are.

And that's how the boy saw his game, a kind of grand illusion. He knew he could play well for his age, better than most of his peers. He knew he could score better than many of the regulars at Old Elm, even as a young teenager. This was fact. But the boy never bragged, never said much about his skills unless asked. His father, however, saw things differently. It was not that his father was boastful. Instead, it was a matter of confidence about his son's talents, and the boy thought that had led to an unrealistic dream. The father was certain his son was going to be a star in high school, would play record-breaking college golf somewhere in Arizona, and turn pro the year he graduated, maybe sooner. His father had the highest of aspirations for a golf career for his son. That was admirable, the boy thought. But unlike the players he watched walk to the 18th green, the boy had his doubts about what he could truly do, what he could honestly be, and misgivings about the life he might lead. It was not that he didn't trust his abilities, or that he lacked the kind of drive needed, or the tenacity for excellence or perseverance. What concerned him was what such a relentless pursuit—one that would be absolutely, unmistakably required—would do to him, if it would forever change the way he might see the game of golf, and the way he might think about his own life.

The boy's family lived in a five-bedroom colonial on a quarter acre. His mother stayed home to raise the kids—he and his younger sister. Dad was a dentist. He, too, had played golf since he was a boy. His father taught him, too. Mom played college tennis and belonged to the Tuesday morning park district league. She made terrific cherry pie and was a member of the PTA when her son was in elementary school. The boy's sister took piano lessons, something he was reminded of most nights when she clunked her way through Mel Bay lessons. The boy received good grades, As and Bs, and classwork came easily. Once on a Halloween Night, the boy was trick-or-treating with friends, and a few of his buddies flipped over pumpkins on a neighbor's porch. The boy wasn't one of them, but he was with them. Guilt by association. Parents were called. The boy couldn't remember another time he had been in trouble. You need to go play in heavy traffic, his golf friend had said to him once. The friend urged him to take more risks, to drop what he saw as his goody-two-shoes take on life. The other boy had had his share of run-ins with teachers and his parents. He got caught smoking and drinking beer in a friend's garage. There might have been some pot. He cut school a few times. Nothing terrible. He simply possessed a more devilish side. Getting in trouble sometimes is good for you, the friend would tell the boy.

The boy wondered often about that. Was he too straight and narrow? Should he go do something dumb, something wrong, something out of the norm? How terrible could that be? It might even be fun. There were times when the boy questioned if golf was one of the reasons he was the way he was. Golf is polite, all the etiquette, all those rules. It is rooted in principle, integrity, and self-discipline. It's the ultimate gentleman's game, the only game where the player can call a penalty on himself, the sport that insists you police your own game, that you never, ever skirt the agreement you have made with the procedures, never fudge the strict guidelines, and if you ever do, dishonor will follow you for the rest of your playing days. Golf demands the straight and narrow and the golf gods are always watching.

A low screamer of an approach hit the front apron of the 18th and skipped across the green to the rear bunker. The pin was in the back half of the green and the next shot would be a tricky one with little room to work with. The boy could hear the conversation.

"Where do you stand?" the partner said as the first player stepped into the trap.

"Five," the partner said. "Putting for bogey." His ball was on the green about 30 feet from the cup.

"Guess I gotta get this one close, then," the first player said. He stood in the sand behind his ball and stared at it for several seconds. "I'm gonna move it," he said.

"You can't move it," the partner snapped.

"Someone didn't rake here. It's in a shoe print."

"Don't care. Play it."

The golfer scowled. "Come on. Seriously?"

"Rules, I'm afraid."

The first golfer shifted his feet in the sand, addressed the ball, took a long backswing and chunked his club into the sand. It was as if the clubhead had hit a wall, suddenly stopping as sand sprayed into the air, the breeze blowing grains into the golfer's face and down the neckline of his shirt. The ball caught the rough at the top of the trap and rolled back in, coming to rest in the crater the golfer had created.

"Unfair," the first player protested.

"Rules," the partner said.

The boy couldn't watch the second and third attempts to get out of the bunker. It was simply too painful to witness. Instead, the boy rested his head on the grass and looked up to the sky. High above the trees, circling with its wings stretched wide, a single hawk, one of several that lived along the fairways, soared against the blue. Inches behind it, another bird—maybe a sparrow or red-winged blackbird, it was hard to tell in the glare of the sun—flapped its wings in an effort to keep pace. As the hawk began to climb, the small bird pulled its wings in tight to its tiny body and landed atop the hawk's tail, riding it in the wind for several seconds.

The boy had never seen anything like that before.

* * *

Early July. It had been an unusually warm day in Fife. Jimmy had finished late after working two rounds, the last with a lawyer from Chicago who carried in his bag a driving iron and an extendable ball retriever, a particular kind of player. He finished with a score somewhere around 105 but Jimmy saw that he had marked his card as an 89. It had been a long day.

In the summer, The Jigger Inn turned touristy, all those rich Americans coming over to play. The old white building sat near the Road Hole and a bagpiper played every night on the patio at sunset, and so it was a popular spot. Caddies came now and then, as Jimmy did, but when it got tight with those on holiday, the caddies cut out. You certainly wouldn't list The Jigger as one of the town's caddie pubs, that's for sure. The pints were a bit expensive. Jimmy, however, stayed. The red-haired girl worked most nights until midnight.

Jimmy stood against the wall near the hearth with a pint of Jigger Ale. He had been there for hours and was several pints deep. The place was humming. No seats to be had, but even if there had been, Jimmy thought it better to stand and let others have a place to rest. He was here most nights, but for many others it was their once-in-a-lifetime experience to be in St. Andrews, and Jimmy loved to watch the expressions on the faces all around, flushed from a day of golf, sea wind, and a night of ale.

The red-haired girl smiled as she worked, the work-smile Jimmy had come to know. It was what she put on to do her job, to serve up pints and drams, laugh at bad jokes, accept flirts, and shrug off the come-ons. Sometime before, she had told Jimmy she was tiring of the work. It was the same thing most nights. Yes, people were having a good time, and many would love to work in a pub like this, she told Jimmy, but the red-haired girl had had her fill. She wanted something new, something else. What that was, she didn't know. She and Jimmy had been together most evenings, and Jimmy wouldn't dare tell himself he had fallen for the red-haired girl. Even if true, he was frightened to admit it. And whenever she began to talk about leaving The Jigger, Jimmy worried that she might also be talking about leaving him. She never said those words, but for Jimmy, it felt like the two were sadly linked. There had been one other girl in Jimmy's world. It was college. They even talked marriage a few times. But in their senior year, she told Jimmy that she thought he had become too much of a dreamer. It broke his heart.

The red-haired girl balanced three full pints on a tray high above her head and squeezed between two tables. Jimmy caught her eye.

"You're good at this, lassie," he said in a laughable Scottish accent.

The red-haired girl rolled her eyes.

Jimmy could have been anywhere while she worked, but he always came to wait out the night. He had his pints and a few drams, and he talked and joked with the golfers about their rounds and told them stories of his caddie escapades—the time a player from Kansas managed to hit three people in one round, including Jimmy, and the story of the old lady from Iowa who fell off the Swilcan Bridge into the burn and broke her ankle. There was the caddie who dropped dead on the 18th tee, and the countless men who insisted they could cut the corner over the hotel on the 17th only to land balls on the roof or hit the big glass window of the upstairs pub. After it shattered multiple times a year, the hotel paid a lot of money to replace the window with special bulletproof glass. Now it only shattered occasionally. Only part of that story was true, but Jimmy told it anyway. The nights at The Jigger were always full of chatter, and laughter, and stories, and drink, but in the end, Jimmy was there for only one reason.

The guys at the table on Jimmy's left had been rowdy most of the night, ordering shots to toast to everything from Old Tom Morris to William Wallace to Mary, Queen of Scots. Like most boisterous bunches, the group was all fun at first, even Jimmy laughed at the old joke about the golfer who skipped his wife's funeral to make his tee time. But after hours had passed, the boys had turned sloppy and handsy.

"Hey sweetheart," one of them said, his beer-less hand grabbing the red-haired girl's wrist as she passed the table. "Bring that nice little rump over here a for a minute."

"Hey," the red-haired girl growled, trying to yank her hand away from the tight grip.

"Just being friendly," he said. "Come on. Be nice."

"Let go of my fuckin' arm," she snarled.

"You know you like us here," he said, nodding to his buddies, "and especially me, right?"

There had been other encounters like this one, and the red-haired girl had handled them with deft skill, tough talk, and a stern "fuck you." Guys backed off. Still, there had been a few times when Jimmy had intervened with threats of his own, getting in the face of a golfer with too many pints in his belly. These few incidents were the only times the red-haired girl had seen Jimmy the slightest bit angry. Jealous, she thought, but jealous at the right time and place. Jimmy knew that this was an unfortunate part of life for a young girl working in a pub in a town packed with men, but for whatever reason, at that moment, on that night, with that guy, Jimmy was not about to let boys be boys.

"Hey, buddy," Jimmy barked. "Back off. Let her go."

"Who the fuck are you?" The guy stood and faced Jimmy.

The red-haired girl had wrangled herself free and moved to the opposite side of the room.

Jimmy, his eyes wide and glaring, wound up and slammed his pint of beer on top of the guy's head. The sound turned heads—a sharp and violent crack like that of a pro's metal driver off the 1st tee. Glass did not break, but beer spewed over Jimmy, the guy, the table, and the floor. Fists flew, tables turned over. The bartender had to pull Jimmy off the offender. There was blood on Jimmy's lip.

Jimmy must have said he was sorry more than a dozen times. Sorry to the bartender. Even sorry to the guy he slugged. Sorry to the red-haired girl. He could not stop saying he was sorry.

"I don't understand," she said as they walked together after midnight along Old Station Road. "You went crazy." The manager had insisted the red-haired girl go home early, and had ordered Jimmy not to come back. His nights at The Jigger Inn were over.

"Are you mad?" Jimmy asked, holding ice wrapped in a bar towel on his cut mouth.

"I don't know what I am," the girl said. "I understand. He was a jerk. But to go after the guy like that?"

Jimmy tried to touch her hair, but she pulled away.

"I didn't like what he was doing." Jimmy said.

"I didn't either," she said, "but, Jimmy, really?"

"Maybe a taste of Balvenie would settle me," he said, grinning. "Dunvegan is still open."

"Jimmy," she whispered. "The drinking. You're drinking a lot. You drank a lot tonight."

"It's a pub," he said. "I want to be with you."

The red-haired girl stopped and turned to look toward the Old Course beyond the short stonewall and into the darkness. The Royal and Ancient Clubhouse, illuminated by its enormous spotlights, sparkled out to the blackness like the king's jeweled crown.

"You know what St. Andrew said about love?" the red-haired girl asked. "When you love someone, you take them into your heart. And that is why it hurts so much when you lose them."

Jimmy and the red-haired girl walked to the flat where she lived with two other girls. At the doorway, Jimmy held the red-haired girl in his arms for many minutes, her head buried in his shoulder.

Whey Pat on Bridge Street served Jimmy a few pints. When the pub closed, Jimmy was not ready to go home. He swayed and stumbled his way along City Road to Howard Place to Hope Street to Windmill Road and stood near the 1st tee of the Old Course, the lights of the R&A casting his shadow before him.

Who are you? What are you doing here?

Jimmy stepped toward the 18th green and onto the fairway, looking out to the night and the rest of the great links. This is the church of golf, he thought, the land of legends and the land of the community, the ancient stretch of dunesland that gave birth to something far bigger and deeper than a simple game. This stretch of ground in a celebrated town had given Jimmy joy, a kind of spiritual balance, and offered him sweet days with a red-haired girl. Too many pints had often made him rather gloomy but combined with the night's fight and the sad goodbye, Jimmy was now consumed by melancholy, yet resolve somehow remained, as if mystics were now guiding him. I don't want to say goodnight to you, he said out loud to the golf course as he walked down the middle of the 18th fairway.

Life is not meant to be lived badly. I will not do that.

Experiences, the good and the bad, are the doors to happiness. Heartache and joy run alongside one another. Love is found and lost, and both feed us. The only constant is where we find ourselves, the land we walk on, this turf, this ancient sandy earth, the sea, and the wind. Life plays out on nature's heavenly spaces. We fail and we prevail. We smile and cry. We are angered and elated. "I believe in angels," Jimmy said into the night.

And they are listening now, hovering above me, watching. And when I fall, they will come and wrap me in loving wings.

Jimmy's walk had brought him to the 17th green and he stood before it. The night's darkness held him, cloaking him in silence. The weather had freshened, and a cool breeze blew off St. Andrews Bay. "I do not want to leave you," he whispered. It was then that he remembered a legend. As the story goes, the bunkers on the Old Course were formed by sheep huddling for shelter from the North Atlantic gales. And a few yards from him on the left side of the green was St. Andrews' most famous, deep as a man is high. From the fairway side, Jimmy peered in. There had been countless times he had schooled players on how to find a way out, to free themselves from the menacing hazard—open the face as wide as possible, swing with purpose, stay down and through. And sometimes he would suggest the easiest way out, swinging away from the green, backward and over the lowest part of the bunker. You only want to escape, he would advise. Get out in one shot before it takes many more. Jimmy smiled thinking about this, the guidance he had given. Sometimes the golfer would give up trying to escape, pick up his ball and throw it out, angry and frustrated. But there were also the times when Jimmy's counsel had worked, the player performed with precision, and the ball floated over the steep sod wall, landing softly and safely on the green. Jimmy loved to see that. He loved the challenge the bunker presented. But more than anything he simply loved looking at it, the intricately layered turf wall and the grainy sand, raked into delicate lines. Even at night, his eyes adjusted to the dark, he could see beauty in its foreboding character, the lure of strength and risk.

Jimmy lowered his left foot into the bunker and steadied himself. With his right still on the turf, he placed his hand against the bunker's low side and climbed in. Standing at the center, he slowly rotated in a tight circle, like a dog before it rests, and gently dropped his body to the sand. Cross-legged and eyes closed, he opened his arms wide to the sky and took in deep breaths, once and then again. Along the breeze, Jimmy could sense the North Sea, briny and potent. He stretched out his legs, rolled on his side, and nestled in tight where the sod met sand, his forearms under his head like a pillow. And in his dreams that night, Jimmy flew high above the ruins of St. Andrews Cathedral and soared through the sea fog to St. Rule's Tower, the medieval beacon for pilgrims lost and searching.

* * *

On the bulletin board outside the pro shop at Old Elm was a list of the scores and names from the club championship last summer, four flights for all levels of player—men and women. The scores for those rounds were to remain posted until the next tournament in late August. The boy stood and read. He knew a handful of the names near the top—Rob Pearson, Steve Lesnik, and always Don Markersman. Markersman was in the championship flight and had posted rounds of 70, 73, 71, and 70 to win the trophy. He'd won it the last two years. He played three times a week and was at the range most every evening. The boy had seen him pounding balls for hours, a real estate agent by profession who did well for himself, allowing flexibility in his day and plenty of time to spend at Old Elm. Word was he was divorced, two grown kids who lived out of state. He didn't say much, only nodded to acknowledge anyone he encountered—the starter, the ranger, other players. Once, he saw the boy hitting practice balls and stood to watch for a time. After a few minutes, he said, "Might want to turn your right foot out about an inch. Helps turn the hips." He nodded and walked away.

A voice came from behind the boy.

"Getting in this year?"

The club pro was an affable guy — older, a bit chunky in the middle, gray hair thinning at the crown. Every day, no matter the weather, he wore the same black wind vest with The Masters logo over the heart. He leaned his shoulder against the frame of the door that led to the shop, his arms crossed at the chest.

The boy shrugged.

"There's a junior flight. But I think you could play in the first flight with a little coaching."

"Not sure."

"It'd be a good test of competitive pressure for your game. Especially if you're going to be on the golf team at school."

The boy wondered where the club pro had heard this. He and his father had been the only ones who had talked about the golf team, at least that's what he thought.

"I've had some conversations with your father," the club pro admitted.

"Oh." The boy had found his answer.

"He thought maybe some lessons would be a good idea. Nothing big, just some tweaks."

"Yeah, well, okay."

"It's summer. You've got time, right? No school. I could work with you. Be fun."

The boy returned to the scores. On the junior list were several names he recognized.

"We'll start slow. Get to know you and your game a bit more."

"Uh huh," the boy said, still reading the names. "I guess."

After a pause, the club pro stepped next to the boy and together they looked at the scores.

"Why golf?" the club pro asked.

"What do you mean?"

"Why not soccer, baseball, even tennis? What a lot of your

friends might be doing. Why golf?"

The boy had never been asked that question, nor had he ever asked himself.

"Just because. I don't know, really."

"Your dad?"

"Well, yeah, he plays."

"What do you like about it?"

Again, the boy had never been asked.

"Well," he said, thinking for a moment. "I like walking."

The club pro laughed. "Walking? That's why you like golf? That's why you come out here?"

The boy rocked his body, putting weight on one foot and then the other, an awkward habit he fell into whenever he was unsure or nervous. A teacher had told him he did that every time the boy gave a class presentation.

"I don't know, the rhythm?"

"The rhythm? What do you mean?"

"It has this, ah, flow? The arms swing and the body turns. It feels good, I guess."

"Tempo."

The boy nodded to be polite, but that was not what he meant. The boy had heard that term tempo. Good players have tempo, and when you're truly good that tempo doesn't waiver. It is always there. But the boy believed it was more than that. Tempo was not exactly the right description of the sinewy, fluid motion he experienced when he hit a golf ball, when he connected square with a 6-iron, heard that sharp click, and watched the ball take flight like a hawk and fall to the turf like a snowflake.

"We can work on tempo," the club pro continued. "We can work on the full swing, chipping, sand game. All of it."

"I have to talk to my dad."

"Sure. Sure," the club pro said. "But he knows. We talk."

"Okay."

"Who's your favorite player?"

"The pros?"

"Yeah," the club pro said. "Let me guess. Tiger."

The boy shrugged.

"Oh, come on," the cub pro said. "Not Tiger?"

The boy didn't want to say. He thought the club pro would laugh again.

"McIlroy? Gotta like Rory, right?"

The pro named a half-a-dozen others, big names of the day, the young studs. But the boy stayed silent.

"Who, then?" The club pro grew impatient.

The boy looked away from the list, down to his shoes, and to the exit door that led to the patio.

"Sam Snead," the boy mumbled.

"What? Snead?" the club pro snickered. "You even know who he is?"

"Wore the hat all the time, the fedora," the boy answered, feeling as if he had been scolded. "Smoothest swing ever. He played golf in his bare feet."

"Never won the U.S. Open, though," the club pro said. "And the bare feet thing, I think that was a story to further his legend."

"You don't like Snead?"

"Oh, he was a great one, sure. Hall-of-Fame. But I'm surprised. Your favorite? Of all the golfers, he's your favorite?"

"Never had a lesson. Completely self-taught. A natural."

"Yeah. Again, that's the legend," the head pro said. "What about courses? I know you haven't played a lot of places, but if you had to pick one or two great ones, where would you go?"

The boy had read about Augusta and Pine Valley. There was Shinnecock Hills and Pinehurst. Pebble Beach had the history and allure. Oakmont in Pennsylvania. Whistling Straits in Wisconsin. There was Chicago Golf Club and Seminole and Winged Foot. Bandon Dunes. But he had always had a special fascination with the courses in Scotland—Muirfield, Turnberry, Royal Dornoch, and especially St. Andrews. A cliché, maybe, but how could the Old Course not be at the top of a golfer's list. No other course had the history and grand myth of seaside land where the world's first golfers walked. In the end, however, despite tradition and legend, the boy could think of no other place he would rather play his golf than where he was standing.

"Really? This place?" The club pro rolled his eyes.

The boy nodded.

"Don't you have dreams, fella?" he asked.

The boy had dreams, but he was certain they were not what others thought they should be. They didn't fall in line with those of his junior golf buddies or what the old timers at Old Elm thought should be the aspirations of a growing boy who played as well as he did. The dreams were not the ambitions of a club champ, the club pro, and they were not his father's dreams.

"We'll work out the details," the club pro said, returning the conversation to the lessons and teaching. "I'll talk to your father. We'll get you all set. It'll be great."

The club pro slapped the boy on the back and returned to the shop. The boy stood before the scoring list, saying the names in his head. He wondered about the players, where they all came from, how they learned to play, how much money had they spent on lessons, or how many dollars on the balls that claim to add another 20 yards to your drive. Did they spend $400 on that new putter, maybe a Scotty Cameron? How about $500 on the new driver? And did either one of those purchases truly make them better, or more importantly, any happier? Maybe for a little while or for a moment. Maybe after one good shot. But how many good shots came after that? And what was a good shot, anyway? One that splits the fairway or one that lands close to the pin, or a putt that drops from 20 feet out? What if you couldn't see the shot, could not gauge its worth on how it ended up? Would there then be any good shots? What about the buttery, effortless sensation of a flawless swing? Doesn't that count? And scores. What have been the lowest scores of these players on this board? How many holes-in-one? So many markers for a golfer, markers that determine worth, whether you are in Flight-1 or Flight-3 of the championship tournament or out playing a round on Saturday afternoon. And there are the money markers, too, the one's that determine where you can play— the city country club with bankers and lawyers, or Old Elm with the mail carriers, the plumbers, and the truck drivers. The boy thought about his father, the dentist. Why hadn't he joined the country club? He certainly had enough money. The boy questioned where his father landed on the golf spectrum. On one hand he wanted his son on the school golf team and on a strict regimen of lessons, but yet Old Elm was where he played his golf, not on the untouchable fairways of the country club, and Old Elm was where his father wanted his son to play his golf, too. The boy was puzzled. Elitist or Everyman? The rich man or the average Joe? In America, whose game was it? The boy was clear about one thing: If all you do as you play this game throughout your life is to seek to play the most exclusive course while striving for the unattainable longest drive or the lowest score, that uncatchable perfection, then you are missing something much more powerful, more significant, more soulful about this game.

"You okay there, slugger?" Nancy from the grill stood near with a turkey sandwich, lemonade, and a frozen Snickers bar, to deliver to the club pro. "You look like you're in a daze or something."

"Nah, just thinking," the boy said.

"By the way," Nancy said, leaning in closer. "I heard the powers that be actually called the police on Jimmy a few days ago."

"Really?"

"The greenskeeper did it. I think the cops are going to patrol a little closer, make sure he doesn't end up on the course again at night. Everyone is watching now."

"He's not hurting anyone or anything."

"A little heavy-handed, don't you think? Hope he doesn't end up arrested or something," Nancy said. "I guess it's trespassing, technically. But why be so rough on him?"

The boy's phone vibrated in his back pocket. "It's my mom," he said, showing Nancy the screen. "Excuse me."

His mother wondered what he had been doing, if he was ready for his ride home. After all, he had been at the course nearly all day. But the boy had other ideas. He wasn't ready to go. Not yet.

* * *

It was one of the newer, younger caddies that found him. The caddie master demanded the newbies get to know the Old Course intimately before handling bags on any regular basis. Seems the caddie, a smart lad from St. Andrews University knew some people, or at least his parents did, at the Royal and Ancient. The caddie master didn't much like handing out caddie jobs to kids with connections, but it happened. Still, the caddie had been warned: Know your stuff or you'll have to go. So, there he was in the misty light before sunrise, walking the course, counting yardages, sketching the undulations of the greens in a little spiral notebook. He was walking the course backward as not to get in the way of the maintenance crews who would soon begin their duties on the outward nine. He came to the 17th green and had begun to step off the yardage from the edge of the road to the high lip of the bunker when he caught sight of a dark shadow. At first, he thought it was an animal, a dog maybe, but as he moved closer to the bunker, he saw it was a man, his legs pulled inward, one arm under his head, another tucked between his knees.

"Jesus Christ?" he murmured. "Jimmy? Jimmy, is that you?"

Without moving, Jimmy opened his eyes, blinked once, and

as if discovering him there should not have been the least bit strange, said, "Good morning."

The young caddie stood at the high edge of the bunker, continuing to speak softly, as if what he was witnessing was a secret to the world. "What the fuck are you doing?"

"Sleeping."

"Have you been here all night?"

"That might've been the best sleep I've ever had."

The young caddie put his hands on his hips and smiled, as Jimmy sat up and stretched out his arms and neck to greet the day.

"How in the hell did you end up here?" the young caddie asked.

"Had a few. Fight with the girl. This seemed the best spot to sleep it off," Jimmy said, standing and brushing sand from his shirt and pants. He looked to the sky and surveyed the links as it, like him, awakened to the day. "This is heaven. Goodness, there is no better place in the universe."

The young caddie looked back along the 17th fairway, and then up toward the 18th tee and green and its traditional white flag. He stood on his tippy toes to see along the road. "No one saw you out here, did they?"

"The air," Jimmy sighed, ignoring the question, "it's so pure."

"Jimmy, are you all right?"

"And my dreams. Oh my. Vivid. Gorgeous. I can't explain it. They were euphoric."

The young caddie stopped asking questions. Jimmy was not interested in answers. The caddie watched as Jimmy stepped from the bunker, walked to the 18th tee, and looked toward the town.

"I was dancing with a woman. Someone I had never seen before. Dancing all along the links here, then down to the beach," he said, describing one of the dreams. "You ever have dreams that, I don't know, send you to some other world, but yet feel so real?"

"We were steaming last night, weren't we?"

"I had a dream of flying, too, over the cathedral. It was total bliss."

"Maybe you should go get some breakfast?"

"Why? I'm not hung over. I'm a little rough around the edges. How am I not sick to my stomach? No headache. Maybe the dreams cured me."

"Aye, sleep can restore us, right?"

Jimmy thought for a moment. "Are you familiar with the Sandman?" he asked.

The young caddie giggled. "What are you talking about?"

Jimmy reminded the young caddie of the mythical character who helped the children fall asleep, who inspired them to dream beautiful dreams by sprinkling sand onto their eyes. It's from a Hans Christian Anderson folktale, Jimmy told him. Ole, the character's name, believed in magic, and he believed in great stories. No one knew more incredible tales than Ole, and no one could tell them as well as he could. Before bed, as the story goes, Ole appears and takes the stairs in his stocking feet, opens the doors to the children's rooms without making a sound, and throws a tiny bit of very fine sand. Not enough to harm the children or hurt their eyes, but enough for them to close their lids and keep their eyes from opening, so the children do not see him. Ole knows that the best stories, the ones that truly matter, are the ones that come in dreams, and so if the children are to experience the prettiest of tales, they must be sleeping. It is only then, in slumber that the mind's most magnificent stories come to life. The Sandman knows this to be true.

"The Sandman got me last night," Jimmy said.

"Or maybe," the young caddie said, resigned now to carry on in the spirit of the moment, "maybe *you're* the Sandman."

Jimmy's smile came slowly, awakening to a revelation. He

liked the sound of that.

Sandman, he thought to himself.

"You did sleep in the sand," the young caddie continued.

"I did, didn't I?"

"And you had all those dreams, like the fairy tale says."

Jimmy looked again down the final fairway. He shook his body as one might do to awaken oneself, shudder oneself into consciousness. And as if he had suddenly realized where he was, he said, "You're the only one who knows I was out here, right?"

Later that day, after a hearty breakfast of bangers, eggs, and tattie scones at the Northpoint Café near the university, Jimmy came to the Old Course looking for a loop. He was worried that word of his overnight accommodations had made the rounds among the caddies and had reached the caddie master.

"Where the fuck you been?" the caddie master growled.

"Sorry. Had some things to do," Jimmy said, anticipating the worst. "But I'm ready to go now, sir."

The caddie master looked him up and down. And in that long silence, Jimmy's heart thumped. He felt it in the back of his throat. Losing the caddie job would be a terrible thing. Being banned from the Old Course would devastate him. What would he do if he were not permitted to walk this land with a bag on his shoulder? Certainly, he could caddie at other links nearby, but losing his connection to St. Andrews, his unwavering and saintly tie to everything the dunesland had given him would be like losing his most faithful friend.

"You know you don't get a loop just because. You have to show up. You have to be here and ready." The caddie master held his rage in check, but it was there, just behind his ruddy face. "Committed. Loyal. This course is your fuckin' wife. This is St. Andrews, for fuck's sake. Do you understand this?"

Jimmy was more than happy to get the talking-to, happy to accept those angry words. It meant the caddie master didn't know, had heard nothing of the story of Jimmy's night in the bunker.

"You're not special," the caddie master continued. "No one is special here, not you, not the old timers, not even me. Nothing is more important than this golf course. Nothing. The gods watch over this place. You think you're bigger than the gods? Fuckin' crap if you think that. Respect. Get some fuckin' respect!"

Jimmy was smiling now. The reprimand was everything he could have hoped for.

"Get that fuckin' grin off your fuckin' face," the caddie master barked, throwing a caddie bib at the target of his disgust, "and get fuckin' prepared."

It was a new day on the Old Course for Jimmy. His walk was fresh, an extra bounce in his step. It was not that he hadn't experienced delight on the course before. Certainly, he had. But this was beyond what he had come to know. His heart remained heavy from the loss of the red-haired girl, and although he had no full-blown hangover, his head whirled a bit from the night's drinking, but the sleep—the magical, restorative, mysterious hours that all living things require—had given birth to a new perception, an unexplained awareness. Those dreams, he thought, had been like presents from some other world, offerings that allowed him to look at everything in a different way. What this new alertness would mean in time, Jimmy was unsure. But at that moment, he simply wanted to believe he had been given a gift.

"And by the way, if drinkin' has anything to do with you being fuckin' lazy today," the caddie master said, "you better get it fuckin' together fast. I don't care how sloppy you get, but when it fucks with me and this course, I'm not happy. Do you get it?"

Jimmy nodded.

"And find some fuckin' chewing gum," the caddie master continued. "Your breath is rank, smells like goat's arse."

Jimmy breathed into his cupped hand and put his nose to his palm. Despite hours of recovery, the big breakfast and a large pot of tea, the foulest part of last night lingered, and it would remain with him for a long time.

* * *

The boy asked Nancy if he could stow his carry bag in the kitchen for a little while, out of sight. He wanted to take a long walk away from the clubhouse and the people, to think, to be by himself. There was a path that looped around the perimeter of the course, near the road, by the small petting zoo, the park district tennis courts, and outdoor basketball court. It was a walking trail mostly under a canopy of trees that few people frequented.

What do I do? How do I figure this out? The lessons, the golf team, Dad. Being young is hard work, he thought. *What am I supposed to do with this life?* An impossible question to answer, but not an unusual one. Still, even in the mix of the boy's personal uncertainties, Jimmy's disappearance was hard to shake. *He's a homeless guy with nothing better to do. Why do I care where he is, what he does, what happens to him? I don't know him from anything. He's nothing to me.* But despite trying to convince himself otherwise, the boy could not let Jimmy go. *He was always nice to me. Never did anyone any harm. And his days at St. Andrews, wow. If that's true, I'm sure he must have great stories to tell.* As the boy walked along the old wooden fence near the sprawling nursing home facility on the hill not far from the 12th fairway, he wondered, too, about Jimmy's health. The boy was certain that whenever Jimmy scratched together some money, he bought booze. Everyone figured as much. Nevertheless, the boy believed Jimmy had to be more than what many at Old Elm thought he was, more than the old clothes, the bad teeth, the scruffy beard, the drink, and the sneaking on the course. Nancy saw it, the boy was certain. There was something sensitive, something in the heart, below the skin, behind the eyes.

Jimmy was Robin Hood, the boy said to himself. That's what he was. He robbed something valuable from those who did not know its true worth and gave it to only those who understood. Not money. Something far more important, like a vision or knowledge. Or maybe he was Huck Finn, the free spirit who had come to see the world's ugliness but chose to believe in the world's goodness. No, the boy thought again. Jimmy was neither. Jimmy was an Argonaut. In school the boy had learned about Greek mythology and the great and arduous expedition to find the Golden Fleece. No one believed this epic tale to be true in all of its various renditions through the centuries, but what most understood was the story's metaphor—a symbol of our own personal journey through life, our own battles with inner failings and troubles. The Golden Fleece is our Holy Grail, our awakening to the universe. The voyage of the Argonauts is the search for truth. And that, the boy now believed, was what Jimmy was—a modern-day Argonaut, a truth seeker.

Still, there was doubt, the kind the real world offers. It was at the farthest point from the clubhouse at the most distant turn in the path that the boy began to question his mythological theory. Maybe, in the end, Jimmy was simply what most people assumed he was—a wayward soul, a bum, a guy who never got it together and never would. The boy did his best to battle against this thought, tried to shake what was an easy and convenient answer. The boy wanted to believe Jimmy possessed something uncommon, something not so easy to understand, as if all his experiences, all that he had become was down a deep well over which a heavy door had been bolted. What about Jimmy's cheers for players, the encouragement he gave? What about his never-missing smile? What about the noticeable joy he showed while watching men, women, and boys play the game he loved? *Do I have that much joy in my life? I have a nice life. I have friends, family.*

What does Jimmy have? What makes him so happy? What makes any of us happy? How does anyone know what it is, happiness? I have a good day on the golf course, shoot a good score, and I'm happy, right? But is that true happiness? Or is it pride, a moment of feeling better than others? That can't be the definition of happiness. Maybe that's Jimmy's secret — maybe he has figured out what happiness is.

When the boy returned to the clubhouse, he was weary, the kind of fatigue that comes from the weight of hard thought. All his energy washed away in a river of wondering.

* * *

Jimmy's loop was for a man from Minnesota who had played the Old Course the first time nine years ago and was back for more. He had come to St. Andrews with his father back then, a Father's Day gift. Now, he was in Europe on business, a software salesman, who had scheduled his travel so he could have the afternoon on the links. Since that first time, the man's father had passed away, so the new round would carry a memory. But along with that came a burning desire to play well, to beat his old score from that earlier time — 95 — and to leave St. Andrews believing he had played his very best.

The weather was good — cloudy and cool but comfortable with a light breeze. The wind was expected to pick up later in the day. There was no rain in the forecast, but one never knows for certain at St. Andrews.

Jimmy introduced himself and shook the man's hand.

"I have a goal today," the man said.

"I do, too, sir," Jimmy said. "But you first, of course."

"I'm going to break my record here today. Yes, it's only the second time I've ever played these hallowed holes. But I will break 95 today and you're going to help me get there."

The man had a brash way about him, confidence that was a little off-putting. But Jimmy had dealt with far tougher personalities than this.

"Well, sir," Jimmy said. "I am at your service."

"Here's what I want you to do," the man said. "I want you to club me and I want you to check my aim. It's hard to judge where best to point your way out here, as you know. And most importantly," the man continued, pausing to be certain Jimmy would hear clearly, "I want you to keep my score but do not tell me where I am at any given time."

"If I may, sir, I think..."

"I am not going to tally any of it," the man continued, reassuring himself of his plan of attack. "I think if I can keep my mind away from the score and let you handle that duty I will focus purely on the shot at hand. One at a time."

"Yes, sir, one shot at a time, but..."

"If I ask you what my score is during the round, do not tell me."

"I wonder if you might consider..."

"Under no circumstances am I ever to know where I am with the score."

"Is that your only goal, sir?" Jimmy asked.

The man cocked his head. "What other goal would there be?"

"This is a magnificent piece of land, a heavenly walk. Might I suggest, sir, that you try to remember where you are as we move about. Breathe in this place. Smell the sea, the wind."

"Now son," the man said, his tone becoming parental, "I am here to break 95."

Jimmy smiled, handing the man his shiny Callaway driver. "You want to hit this on the left side. Plenty of room. Can you hit it about 230 or so?"

"I think I can, yes," the man said. "New club just for this day." He waved the driver in the air to show it off.

Jimmy was certain it was more likely that the man could hit his driver 210 at best. No one ever hits the ball as far as they think they can. Plus, Jimmy had quickly assessed the man's game, evaluating his clubs—cavity back irons, two hybrids— and his practice swing, a less-than-fluid, outside-in motion.

"Stay left and we'll avoid the burn," Jimmy said. "Do you mind if I give you some course history as we play?"

"Don't need it. Don't want it. I know this hole is named Burn because of the creek. I know the water runs right in front of the green. I know all that."

As the man teed his ball and stepped behind to set up his shot, he asked, "By the way, you said you had your own goal out here. What is it?"

"Ah, no matter, sir. My goal is your goal," Jimmy knew it was not the time to offer his personal musings, not after being scolded when he tried to offer another side of the adventure and to convey a course fact or two. "Oh, and by the way, sir," Jimmy continued after a pause. "They call me Sandman out here. You can call me that if you like."

"Okay, Sandman," the man said, addressing the ball. He waggled once, twice, and with a hefty lunge, he struck the ball, sending it high and left. It caught the fairway, bounced several times, and settled on the turf. "That'll work. About 250. I'll take it."

"Beauty, sir," Jimmy said. The man's coming approach shot would allow for a good look at the pin, but his ball, Jimmy was certain, had traveled only about 200. Jimmy knew every spot and every angle of the Old Course, knew every yardage, but he had learned from many a loop never to douse the delusions of a golfer who believed he had done his best, no matter how far off his reality.

"So, Sandman. How'd you get that name?" the man asked as they stepped off the tee.

"Oh, just a name someone gave me one day," Jimmy said, returning the man's driver to his bag. "Long story."

Jimmy and the man had been paired with another player. He was from Japan and spoke no English. His caddie was one of the old timers who had carried for hundreds of players. He spoke no Japanese. But he knew how to handle just about anyone from anywhere. It was if he had some secret unspoken way to communicate. Because of this, there would be little interaction between the players or the caddies. Maybe a helping look at a putt or two, but that would be it. For the most part, Jimmy and the man from Minnesota were alone together, on a mission.

A par at the 1st hole set things off on the right path. The man noted this as he walked from the green, but then reminded himself he was not going to tally his strokes, only Jimmy would do that. At the 2nd, the long par-4, the man chunked two in a row, but he stayed true to his strategy and did not ask Jimmy his score when the hole was completed. On the 3rd, he had a burst of confidence when he made a twisting 15-foot putt. And at the 4th, he stood on the tee box and looked out toward the fairway, its brownish hues now clearly evident in the afternoon sun.

"That scrub out there, I can carry that, right?" the man asked.

Jimmy was certain he could not. The scrub sits in the middle of the fairway and only a truly excellent shot can send the tee ball over it safely.

"I think if you stay right, you'll have a better approach," Jimmy said.

"Hmm. You know what? I think I got this." With that, Jimmy handed the man his driver, believing it best not to debate the miscalculation.

The man produced a mighty swing, grunting and falling back on his heels, nearly losing his balance. The ball set out on a low line drive, bouncing once, then again, and disappearing.

The other player's caddie shook his head. "I'm afraid you're in the shit," he said.

The man was silent, not removing his eyes from the fairway for several moments.

"What the hell?" the man said, now glaring at Jimmy.

Jimmy reached for the man's driver and said, "We'll find it. Maybe you can get a club on it and advance it. Let's take it from there."

"Damn it, Sandman," the man said under his breath. "You've got to keep me in line. Watch my aim. Got it? Jesus."

"Lot of golf, sir. Lot of golf to play," Jimmy said.

The other player hit his tee ball and kept it short and right, the more prudent way to go. Jimmy congratulated him on a good shot. This produced a scowl from the Minnesota man. Jimmy smiled sheepishly. As they walked off the tee box, Jimmy began to tell the story of how the 4th had been given its name.

"In the nineteenth century, a local used to have a refreshment cart out here and he sold plenty of ginger beer," Jimmy said. "That's why it's called Ginger Beer."

The Japanese man nodded with unknowing interest, as he certainly understood none of what Jimmy had to say. The Minnesota man turned away, his teeth clenched, his face reddening.

"It's quite a story of how this place is truly the town's public land, the land of the people," Jimmy continued. "One of the wonderful things about St. Andrews and it…"

"Shut the fuck up, Sandman," the Minnesota man growled. "Fuck course history. *I'm* your focus. Now let's find my ball."

The tee shot was deep in wiry, high grass. Jimmy handed the man his wedge.

"I can't get home from here with this," the man insisted.

"You want to get out of that gnarly stuff and set yourself up for the next shot," Jimmy said. "For now, this is your best plan. Let's take our medicine and live to swing again."

"Absolutely not," the man said. "Give me my 4-iron."

"Sir, you asked me to club you. And yes, the game is played on the ground here, 7-irons and the like. But you must get out of the mess you're in and a 4-iron won't do this for you here, sir."

"This is a long-ass hole. I need my 4-iron."

Three swings later, the man's ball had still not found the putting surface. His last shot hit the big mound in front of the green and checked up. A bump and run with his 7-iron— Jimmy's strongly suggested shot—eventually landed the ball where the man could putt it, but it took three more strikes to find the cup. For several holes afterward, the man snubbed Jimmy, walking quickly to the next shot. Jimmy tried smiling as he clubbed him, but the man continually avoided Jimmy's eyes and said not a word.

The 8th is one of only two par-3s on the course. In front is a bunker that catches dozens of shots each day. The hole turns against the wind on that end of the links and Jimmy could feel the breeze freshening.

"It measures 160 today, sir," Jimmy said, handing the man his hybrid.

"Come on, seriously?" the man grumbled.

"The wind, sir. You will need more club. Play what the course gives you."

"I'll fly it."

"The wind is your friend, sir."

The man rolled his eyes and took the club in his hands. As he placed his tee in the ground, he asked, "Where am I right now? What do I have at this point?"

"Sir, you asked me not to."

"I didn't mean any of that. Tell me."

"Sir. You insisted."

The man shook his head. "Sandman, come on. You're into this spiritual Zen shit, aren't you?"

Jimmy smiled with his eyes.

"Thought so," the man said, addressing the ball. "This better not go over the back."

The swing produced a sweet snap, indicating a good strike. Both the man and Jimmy watched as the ball lifted high to the right side, bounced in front of the putting surface, and vanished from view.

"Is that on?" the man asked.

Jimmy reached for the club. "Well done, sir," he said.

"I'm on, then?"

"Putting, sir."

"I knew that was at least a two-club wind. I knew it. I just knew it."

"Yes, you did, sir. Yes, you did."

The man's play after the turn was steady. During the first holes of the inward nine, Jimmy could see the man's sureness building but along with it were moments of unease. He asked if his shots were safe, if they were playable, especially when he couldn't see the landing areas clearly. More clouds had formed but still no rain. And Jimmy could detect from the colors of those clouds, their layers of gray, that rain would not be an issue for the remainder of the round. It had become gusty, however, as was predicted and as it often did at the Old Course. With this, Jimmy knew the man's anxiety would only build.

"The wind here is a beautiful thing," Jimmy said, standing on the 14th tee. "It's as much a part of this land as the sea and the turf. If you accept this, you can weather it."

"This hole is a bear," the man said, looking out to the fairway of the Old Course's longest hole.

Long, as the hole was named, could measure out more than 600 yards, but for amateurs it was playing at 570, still a hefty distance.

"Do you see the church steeple? Far along the horizon?" Jimmy asked. "That's your aiming point. Your target is God, if you will." Jimmy smiled, hoping to ease the man's mounting fears with a bit of light humor.

"But then there's Hell out there, too," the man said, referring to one of the course's fiercest hazards, Hell Bunker. It is a monstrous hole in the ground, 300 square feet of sand and seven feet deep. If one's ball ends up there, consider it in the belly of the beast.

"Nothing to worry about," Jimmy said. "No concerns on your tee shot and we'll work around it when we get there. It's all about managing."

"God or Hell. What a hole," the man groused.

Jimmy handed the man his driver. "Smooth, like butter," he said. "Don't force it. Nothing forced ever turns out well."

The man teed his ball, stood behind it, closed one eye as if aiming a rifle, and using his club, pointed toward the steeple.

"I think I need to know before I hit this," the man said, his eyes away from Jimmy. "Five holes to go. I should know where I stand."

"Sir, you explicitly told me," Jimmy said.

"Screw it. Tell me."

"Sir?"

The man slammed his club head to the turf. "Okay, okay. Forget it. Never mind. Damn it."

Jimmy grinned and gave a thumbs-up. "Remember, like butter," he said.

The man's drive was the best of the day, the ball traveling nicely down the left side of the fairway. Still, navigating the rest would be the most challenging.

Neither Jimmy nor the man said a word as they marched up the fairway. The man's mind certainly on what he had left to face, confronting one of the toughest holes in the world, and reckoning with the inner impulses to calculate his score. He ticked off the holes in his head, counting silently. *What did I have at the 4th? Was it a 5 on 10?* Not all of it was clear or certain, but he knew he must be close. And now, should he or should he not take the risk?

Standing before his ball, his hands on his hips, the man squinted to see what remained. Jimmy sat the bag down and pulled a club.

"Hit this," Jimmy said, handing the man his 6-iron, grip first.

The man stared at the club for a moment, then at Jimmy. He sighed, looked down the fairway and back to Jimmy. "Three-wood," he demanded.

"Sir, you asked that I club you," Jimmy said. "I highly suggest the 6."

"Three-wood," the man said, again.

Jimmy replaced the iron and lifted the wood. "I know you hit this well, but this may not be the time."

The man stood behind his ball, addressed it, waggled the club twice, and launched an intense whack. The ball whistled. It was a good strike. You could hear it in the contact. But Jimmy knew. He knew what the outcome would be and reached out for the man's club without bothering to witness the ball coming to rest. The ball's fate was undeniable.

"Am I in?" the man asked. "I'm in, aren't I?"

"What's done, is done, sir. Acknowledge it and let's face the here and now."

"Fuck," the man snarled.

The ball sat in a flat portion near the bottom of Hell Bunker. The man was lucky. If it had been closer to the bunker's sod wall, Jimmy would have suggested he hit his third shot backward to avoid any possibility of leaving it in the sand. Instead, Jimmy handed the man his sand wedge and told him to take a solid, lengthy swing.

"Remember this, sir. If you hit this club, and find your easiest way out, you will be able to say you have been to Hell and back."

The man stepped into the deep hole and looked up at Jimmy, as if he had been abandoned there, missing in action, and unfindable.

"Sir, if I might," Jimmy said. "This is a good opportunity to consider this extraordinary moment. One of the Old Course's most notorious hazards has engulfed you. Most people stand where you are and believe they are hopeless. Some are angry, frustrated with their game. They have spent a lot of money to travel to this magnificent land, but here they are at the bottom of a crater, befuddled. But it is not the time for anger. Instead, it's time to embrace the experience. For you are here, at golf's Mecca, its oldest and most beloved links, the turf of the fairways, the gorse, the wispy rough, and yes, this bunker. This, too, this Hell of a bunker is one of golf's treasures."

The man shook his head, as if to admonish Jimmy's words, then took his stance and his swing, and lifted his ball free, out of its prison. He finished the 14th with another bump-and-run and two putts. Nothing was said through the next several holes, not a single word between the man and Jimmy or to the other player or his caddie until they stood on the 17th tee.

"The good players take it over the edge of the hotel," the other player's caddie said. "No one here today should be attempting such foolishness."

The Japanese player nodded and hit his drive far left. Still in play but creating a much longer hole.

Jimmy furnished the man's driver. "Stay left, sir. We are going to play this like a three-shot hole. Take our time and enjoy the ride."

The man stood behind his ball. "Three-shot hole. That must mean I have some wiggle room on that score, right? But you're not going to tell me, are you?"

"Let's appreciate your final holes. We don't know when you will return to this place."

After a long fairway wood and a punched 7-iron as his approach, the man had landed his ball on the putting surface. The flag was up front and that kept the Road Hole Bunker out of play. Still, the deep and famous trap lured both players and they took a long gaze at it.

"It's destroyed many a player," the other caddie said.

"Ah, yes, but don't you think it's such a beautiful thing?" asked Jimmy.

No one agreed.

The final hole at St. Andrews reminds anyone who walks it, more than any other on the course, that the links belongs to the old town. It is the most photographed golf hole in the world— the Royal and Ancient clubhouse in the distance, the Swilcan Bridge ahead, and there along the right side near the green, a number of the centuries-old stone buildings of St. Andrews. For several minutes, there was not a word. The four of them stood and regarded what was before them.

Finally, Jimmy spoke. "We are at the last, a hole that gives pause. Drivable for some, but yet in front of the green is the notorious Valley of Sin."

"Purgatory for the man who risks too much, wouldn't you say?" the other caddie said, smiling, not expecting an answer.

"I suggest a hybrid to the left side and a short iron in," Jimmy said.

"Look, Sandman," the man whispered as he leaned into Jimmy. "Let's get real. Put all that earlier talk aside. Let's forget that. Now is the time to tell me. I must be close. Where do I stand?"

"Sir," Jimmy said, handing him the suggested club, "that is the last thing a wise man should be thinking about now. You stand before the final tee shot on this holy ground. Give thanks for being here and make a steady swing that'll take you home."

"I'm really tired of your bullshit spiritual crap," the man said. He snatched the club from Jimmy's hand. "Let's get this over with."

The tee ball landed safely, and the man's approach shot managed to fly the Valley of Sin and come to rest on the right side of the green. A long lag putt placed the ball three feet from the hole.

The other golfer made his final putt and now Jimmy's man was preparing for his.

"Going to tell me now?" the man asked as he crouched and

eyed the line.

"Left edge and firm," Jimmy said.

The man shook his head, addressed the ball, exhaled, and struck it. It fell in dead center.

"Well done, sir," Jimmy said.

"So?"

"Sir?"

"Score. What was it?"

"Did you enjoy the experience, sir?"

"What was my score?" the man asked again, his tone more urgent.

"And do you think you might return someday?"

"Son-of-a-bitch! What did I have?"

Jimmy plucked the ball from the cup, reached to take the man's putter, and looked directly at him. "I'm not sure," Jimmy said.

The man's face reddened; his jaw jutted forward.

"What are you fucking talking about?" His voice was low, slow, guttural.

"I don't truly know the score," Jimmy continued. "Score is immaterial. It is not why we play. Score is for tournaments. It's for sport. Golf, the game you and I play, is not about that. Score is a false and misguided goal."

"You have to be fucking kidding me," the man barked. "Get out the scorecard. Let me see it."

Jimmy handed him the card. It was blank.

"You were asked specifically to keep my score." The man's voice cracked as he walked at Jimmy's side, waving the empty scorecard. "What the fuck is wrong with you?"

"I only hoped to give you another way to understand this game."

"You're an idiot," the man snarled. "I'm reporting you. You should be reprimanded. Fired."

The other caddie and player quickly walked away, hoping

to avoid being pulled into the confrontation, but the argument was impossible not to notice. Tourists standing at the back of the green watched as it unfolded, and now, the caddie master had heard the man's raised voice and was marching toward it.

"What might be the problem here?" the caddie master asked, attempting to remain calm.

"Are you the boss?" the man asked.

"I am the caddie master, yes, sir."

In a furious tirade, the man insisted he had been disobeyed, wronged, duped. He protested what he called Jimmy's "Zen golf nonsense" and questioned how such a "clueless man" could be a caddie at the world's greatest golf course. The man continued, punctuating his outburst with flailing arms as the caddie master listened, glaring at Jimmy after each angry sentence. Exhausted, the man stood silent, clenched his teeth, snatched his bag from Jimmy's grasp, marched toward the walkway, and was soon out of sight.

Jimmy had remained meditative throughout, saying nothing in his defense. And as the caddie master stood before him now, Jimmy removed his bib.

"I'm certain it's all over, now. I am finished here," Jimmy said.

The caddie master sighed, looked out toward the course, and in a composed and steady voice said, "There comes a time when every young man must decide if he is going to live an unconventional life or become part of the rest of the world."

"Sir?"

"Heard melodies are sweet, but those unheard are sweeter," he said. "It's Keats. An Englishman, but a good one."

"I'm not sure I understand," Jimmy said.

"What we dream of being, laddie, is sometimes more marvelous than what we are experiencing, the life we are living at the moment," the caddie master explained. "Dreaming of a life and following that dream, even if it gets us nowhere is sometimes sweeter than reaching it."

"Yes, sir."

"Don't misunderstand," the caddie master continued. "I am not happy. You did not fulfill the duties as we expect here at St. Andrews. You will no longer caddie at the Old Course. But I understand what happened here."

The caddie master's unforeseen introspection had astounded Jimmy. He thought maybe the old man had missed something, failed to comprehend fully what had transpired. But the caddie master had only needed the right time to allow this side of him to be witnessed.

"I was you once," the caddie master said. "Idealistic, believing in the mystic nature and power of this game, and that it somehow holds a spiritual connection to the land, maybe even to godliness. I once believed in the unconventional life, too."

The caddie master spoke of his younger days when he considered remaining a simple caddie forever, walking the land every day, enjoying the company of like-minded souls, sharing pints and stories, and accepting and enjoying whatever golf and life gave him. Jimmy listened closely, astonished that he was not being more harshly admonished. He understood the dismissal. Saddened by it, yes. But the caddie master's confessional, Jimmy could never have imagined.

"There comes a crossroads when a principled young lad must decide his path. Living outside the norms of the world takes courage and forthrightness. Living inside the lines is easy. You go to public school, you listen to your mum, you find a job, you marry your best lassie, you stay out of trouble, you raise a good family, and you go to church. Here in St. Andrews, we live inside the lines. Not that it is a terrible thing. For it is not. There is goodness in convention and tradition. I'm proud of this and what we are here."

"I am, too, sir," Jimmy said. "But I believe I have experienced something beyond this, it seems. It came to me suddenly, like in a dream."

"You are at that crossroads," the caddie master continued, "and you have chosen the other road."

"I believe so," Jimmy whispered. "At least for now."

"Aye, go ahead, embrace it. But know what this means," the caddie master continued. "How far outside society's norms are you willing to go? What demons are you avoiding and which ones will be forever with you now that you have made this choice? You can return to the traditions. It's not unheard of. But at this time, you must be ready for the unconventional life. Freedom, as has been said and sung, means having nothing left to lose."

For several hours, Jimmy walked aimlessly through the streets of St. Andrews. He spoke with no one along the way, entered no pub, but after some time found himself inside a small book and gift shop on Bell Street. On the counter was a sterling silver St. Andrew cross and chain. Jimmy was drawn to it, how it reminded him of this beloved town—the town he would soon leave behind—the ancient cathedral a three-minute walk away, and his transformative dream in the sands of the Road Hole Bunker. Jimmy spent 30 quid, nearly all the money in his pocket. He placed the cross around his neck and as he exited the shop, the shopkeeper reminded him of an old Scottish superstition. "The cross will keep away evil—the witches and the wicked angels. It will serve you well. Wear it always, lad," he said. With that, the shop's door was locked, and Jimmy stepped again into the St. Andrews night to go back home.

* * *

The boy sat on the wooden bench at the entrance to the Old Elm clubhouse, his bag at his side, as his mother pulled the car into the turnaround. She waved to her son through the window. The boy stood, threw his bag strap over his right shoulder, paused, and looked out toward the 1st tee.

"Honey, you coming?" his mother asked.

The boy did not answer.

"Honey?"

The boy thought about his father, the golf team, and the lessons. And Jimmy.

"Did Dad ever know that guy on the 5th hole?"

His mother did not understand.

"Dad, when he played out here, did he ever meet Jimmy?"

"I know he's played with a lot of fellas here, maybe someone named Jimmy."

"No, not someone he played with. This is the homeless guy on the 5th hole who always hangs out."

"There's a homeless man hanging around the golf course?" his mother asked.

"His name is Jimmy. He's always there. Now he's not."

"Well, you know how some of these people are. Maybe someone has come to help him."

"They kicked him off the course."

"Maybe they should have. Probably not good to have a homeless man roaming around the course."

"He's different."

"I'm sure he is, honey. There are services and shelters. Are you coming?"

The boy lifted the bag from his shoulder and balanced it against his side. Above him he heard the call of a hawk, the high-pitched cry. He could see it soaring with its wings spread wide, and behind it, a red-tailed blackbird, chasing.

"Did you ever see that?" the boy asked his mother.

"See what?"

"The hawk," the boy said, pointing.

The blackbird found the hawk's tail and like what he had seen earlier that day, it held on for the ride.

"The hawk and the small bird," the boy continued. "Do you

see it? It's like they understand each other, like they're playing together, like partners."

His mother strained her neck to see out the window, but the birds were too high now, flying over the clubhouse to the west where she couldn't see.

"That's nice," she said. "Come on. Let's get going."

The boy watched until he could no longer see the birds.

"Mom," he said, "when did Dad talk to the pro here about lessons?"

"Oh, I'm not sure. A few weeks ago, maybe, I guess," she answered. "I have dinner at home waiting for you. Let's talk about this in the car."

"But he never talked to me."

"I'm sure he will."

The boy sighed and looked at his phone to mark the time.

"I think I'm going to stay a bit longer," the boy said.

"Honey?"

"Juniors can play now for free on the front nine."

"The sun will be down before you can finish," his mother insisted. "Let's go home."

"Mom, please. I want to do this."

After more back and forth, the boy's mother agreed. Maybe he needed this, she thought. And, in the end, what could be wrong with a boy playing golf as the sun falls on a summer day?

"Be sure you are right here at this spot when you're finished," his mother said.

From the car window, the boy's mother could see her son's eyes, clear and blue, like his father's. He was getting bigger by the day, taller, his shoulders wider than a few months ago. His brown hair, thick like his grandfather's as a young man. It was in need of a trim, a tight summer cut overdue. There were a few wispy stubbles of facial hair along his chin line and under his nose. The boy had begun shaving, but the grooming was, at best, once a week. His mother recalled when the boy was only a toddler, how he loved to splash in the blow-up pool in the yard, giggling as the water flew into the air. There was the elementary school holiday pageant when he played an elf, even then too tall for the part. She remembered how he used to hit a Wiffle ball off a plastic tee, chasing it, over and over again for hours. And she recalled his first time striking a golf ball in the open field near the schoolyard with a cut-down wedge his father had fashioned. After hours had passed, the boy's hands had become red and chaffed, but he never said a word about it, never complained.

His mother pulled away, smiling and waving, and the boy headed for the 1st tee at Old Elm.

* * *

Turkey lunch meat remained in the refrigerator, and a delivery of fresh bread was scheduled for the next morning, so using up what was left was a good idea. Nancy placed two slices in the toaster and retrieved the brown mustard and mayo packets, and a few dill chips from a jar. When the bread popped, Nancy layered the turkey on one piece, and spread the condiments on the other. After placing the pickles on top, she positioned the bread slices together, cut the sandwich diagonally, and wrapped it neatly in aluminum foil. In a brown bag, along with the sandwich, she included two lunch-sized bags of potato chips and a packet of orange peanut butter crackers. From the cooler, she pulled an Arnold Palmer, placed it in a double plastic bag of ice and tied it closed.

It had been several days since she had stopped by with food for Jimmy, the last time she saw him, and now with what had transpired, he might not be there at all. Nancy was going anyway, as she had done many times before. After the grill closed an hour before sundown, as it always did, Nancy would do what she had promised. And if Jimmy was not in his usual spot and nowhere to be found, Nancy would place the food in another bag and leave all of it by the tree. If Jimmy returned, it would be there. And if not, she knew the squirrels would get to it eventually. That would not be a terrible thing, she thought. But she prayed Jimmy would find it first, that he would return, and that he was all right.

As Nancy placed everything in the refrigerator, a twosome came in from the 9th green, heading out for as much of the back nine as they could play before sundown.

"Some bottled water, please," said one player.

"I'll take a Coke and a lot of ice," said the other.

"You got it, boys," As Nancy tallied the purchases, she asked, "Did you see Jimmy at the 5th when you came through?"

"The homeless guy?" the first player asked. "I heard he's gone for good. Course wants him out of there."

"You didn't see him?" Nancy asked.

"Nope," said the second player.

Nancy handed the players their change.

"Ever talk to the guy?" Nancy asked.

"I've said hello, sometimes, that's about it," the first player said. "He seemed harmless."

"Gave me a good tip once," the second player said to the first. "Never asked. But he gave it anyway. My putting stroke was too long, he told me. I shortened it. Started putting better. That was last year, I think."

"Wasn't he a pro or something once?" the first player asked.

"No. Not Jimmy," Nancy answered.

"Do you know him?"

"Everyone knows Jimmy in some way or another," Nancy said. "A little Jimmy in all of us, don't you think?"

The players nodded politely, unsure of what Nancy had meant or what to make of what she said. The two men thanked her and headed for the 10th tee. Nancy locked up the grill and exited carrying the food and drink.

* * *

"If you see that son-of-a-bitch out there, call the cops," the greenskeeper told the two members of the late-day crew. "Before you call it a night, let's rake those traps from the 1st fairway on through, as much as you can get done. And again, if you see him, I want you to call the police."

The crewmembers knew of Jimmy. They never found him to be a problem.

"If he's on the golf course again, walking around, acting weird, nail him. I can't have that anymore. I'm tired of it," the greenskeeper continued.

Most didn't see what the big deal was if Jimmy spent time on the course in the dark when no one was playing and no one could see, but the greenskeeper's job was to maintain the playing surface and keep it in the best shape it could be. Recently, there had been some teenagers who rode a dirt bike across a green, tearing it up, and another time a bunch of kids held a beer party on the 4th hole in the dead of night. Dozens of beer cans littered the fairway, and it took several weeks and new sod to repair the damage.

"What did the cops do with him last time?" one worker asked.

"Warning, probably. It's what they do," the greenskeeper said. "I don't care. Just keep him away. If he was drunk, maybe they threw him in jail for a night, sent him to rehab. God, I fuckin' hope so. I don't want him here again."

"I don't want to argue or anything, but the golf course is part of the park district and the city, right?" the second worker asked.

"What's your fuckin' point?" the greenskeeper snapped.

"Public land."

"Public land, my ass! This is my golf course."

"Hey, okay. Not trying to start a fight," the worker said.

"No excuses," the greenskeeper growled. "And remember to rake those traps in a circular motion, I want to see those pretty fuckin' lines in the sand."

The workers placed their rakes in the back of the maintenance cart and headed for the course.

* * *

The night before the early morning when Jimmy was found in the bunker on the 5th at Old Elm, before the greenskeeper called the police, Jimmy had been dreaming. It was a familiar dream, an old friend of a dream—flying over St. Andrews Cathedral, soaring in the wind from the sea. Even after all the years, the dream came to him from time to time and it made him happy when it did. Before he rested in the sand that early morning, he was walking barefoot on the fairway, as he had done before. However, this time was different. This time he was taking stock of where he had been.

When he returned home from Scotland years ago, Jimmy went to work helping to build houses on the east side of town. He had no carpentry skills. His job was to carry 2x4s and lug drywall from the trucks. Grunt work was what was needed. Grunt work was what he gave them. Jimmy didn't mind the hard labor. And he enjoyed the after-work beers at the tavern with the guys from the carpentry crew. They worked hard and played hard. Jimmy spent many months trying to forget about golf, St. Andrews, and the red-haired girl. When it became too much, and it did sometimes, he would caress the St. Andrew cross and rub it like a magic charm.

Come late autumn, Jimmy had had enough. It wasn't that he didn't like the work. It was more about the monotony, the urge for a change. His father offered him money to go back to school. His mother suggested a trade—electrician or plumber or maybe a carpentry apprenticeship now that he had some experience with home builders. Jimmy was not interested. He received an old Jeep Cherokee from his uncle—a four-door wagon—and he set off to travel. He had saved some money and believed if he headed out, taking side jobs here and there, maybe even caddying a few places along the way, he could keep moving for a long time.

Jimmy headed south toward North Carolina with Pinehurst as his destination. On the rural roads south of Durham, he saw farmers in the tobacco fields and on the porch of a weather-beaten farmhouse, two old Black men sitting on the steps in the shade. They looked tired and beaten. He stopped at a small roadside restaurant and ordered sweet tea and peach pie from a young woman who carried pain in her face. She, too, was weary. Even at her tender age, Jimmy could see she had lost some level of hope. Jimmy caddied at Pinehurst for six weeks before he simply failed to show up one morning.

He considered heading for Augusta, but he knew he wouldn't have much chance of landing a caddie job there, not when Augusta National, of all places, would certainly check his job history and discover the reason he was dismissed at St. Andrews and that he had disappeared at Pinehurst. And on top of this, Augusta was the height of the rich and privileged, the elitist and entitlement of the American version of the game that went against the Everyman sensibility of Scotland and what Jimmy had come to believe was golf's true roots. He traveled farther south and found work at a restaurant in Pensacola, washing dishes. He slept in his Jeep and washed-up each day in the restaurant's bathroom. It wasn't long before he was on his way again, finding caddie work at Bay Hill outside Orlando, closing his eyes to the fortunate and advantaged long enough to make some money and believe again in the contemplative nature of a good walk. But, in time, Jimmy was on the road once more.

Heading west, Jimmy now believed there was a mysterious force fueling his journey, helping him stay out of trouble through the speed traps, keeping the old Jeep from breaking down, and assisting him in finding cheap motels and abandoned parking lots to rest and sleep. It was good on the road. Nothing to interfere, only healing landscapes — pines in Alabama and the wide, lonely plains of Texas. In New Mexico, he found work at a chile farm, tending to the fields. He learned a bit of Spanish and thought he had fallen in love with a beautiful black-haired Mexican girl. Months later Jimmy arrived in Las Vegas. He caddied at Shadow Creek for a time and worked nights at a rundown casino outside of town where he tricked the manager into believing he knew how to operate a roulette table. While he had the job, Jimmy was permitted free drinks each night after his shift. One morning the previous night caught up with Jimmy and he never worked at Shadow Creek again, and left Las Vegas behind.

On the long drive to Carmel, Jimmy talked to himself. "This is what I wanted," he said out loud. "This is the unconventional life. Travel. Freedom. No ties." Jimmy reminded himself over and over as if trying to convince himself that what he was doing was the right thing. Unconventional. On his own, for sure. But something was missing, and he knew it. What he had discovered unexpectedly in St. Andrews had been lost in the fog of the everyday. "St. Andrew, can you give me a little help out here?" Jimmy wondered, caressing the cross. At a gas station near the California border, while pumping fuel, he retrieved the old photo he had stuffed in his pocket before the journey began and held it in his hand. The red-haired girl was so far away.

It took some doing, but Jimmy ended up working at the Pebble Beach Resort. He cleaned rooms at night at the hotel. During the day, he would sit under the cypress tree that guards the 18th green and watch the golfers find their way home. It was there that he got to know some of the caddies and hoped he might find a way to a job carrying a bag. He telephoned the club and showed up at the caddie station several times a week, hoping to get a chance to interview. Walking Pebble every day would surely balance his emotional teetering, he thought. Pebble was expensive to play. But it was a public course, open to everyone and anyone who could find the money. The place might return him to the path he had been on but had lost somewhere in his long journey. Still, despite what he wanted, despite his desires and tenacity, Jimmy never had a chance at Pebble. Maybe his reputation preceded him. Maybe his luck simply ran out. Maybe through it all he had found that the unconventional life was a lie.

After giving up on Pebble, Jimmy arrived in Oregon. He worked for a logging company for a time, helping to keep the machines oiled and gassed for the work in the forests. In Sisters, he bussed tables at Takoda's Bar. Halfway to Helena, the Jeep broke down. He worked at a service station for three weeks to pay for the transmission repair. Then it was Cheyenne, Denver, and Kansas City. Several weeks in one town and then gone to the next. Money was low and work was sparse, and Jimmy spent too much on drinking. It was on the drive to Chicago through St. Louis that the realization came over him, the true understanding that he might never find whatever it was he was looking for. He admitted it to himself along I-55 somewhere near Springfield. Why on this highway and why then was difficult to answer, but the clarity of what he would no longer have was apparent. "The only thing I truly loved was walking the links at St. Andrews," Jimmy said aloud as he drove. "Carrying a bag, smelling the sea, sleeping in the sand." And it was then that Jimmy knew that he would never again have the chance to return to Scotland, to golf's home, to the place he believed he could have stayed forever.

When a man takes on the belief that he must, with all his heart, lead an unconventional life, he too must admit that there is risk, the real chance that he will never find whatever it is he longs for. There is an inherent gamble in such a pursuit.

Knowing what an unconventional life truly is, is also the puzzle to happiness. Such a life can be a genuine mission but accepting all of the hazards is also part of it, a part not found in the alluring romanticism, the very aspect that draws a man to it. To live unconventionally may be beyond most of us, beyond our capabilities. It is a heavenly quest, and maybe, in the end, that is enough.

In Goshen, Indiana, Jimmy sold the old Jeep for $500 to the owner of a car repair shop, hitchhiked for days, sleeping in farm fields and on rest stop benches, and arrived in his hometown on a clear spring night. His parents wanted him to stay at the house, to feed him a good meal, and to sleep in his old bed in his boyhood room, but Jimmy had come to prefer the outdoors, and from that time forward, it would always be the open air for Jimmy, alone, on his own, under the sky in the town where he grew up.

* * *

The day's early breeze had calmed, and the boy could see that the flag was still. There was no one on the fairway and no one on the green. The hole was wide open.

"Looks like the course is yours," the starter said from his seat in the cart. "You know you won't finish the front before dark."

The boy smiled.

"Getting in some practice then, huh?" the starter continued.

"Something like that," the boy said.

The boy's drive sailed along the right side, landing on the downslope of the fairway and kicking left to the middle. He threw his bag on his shoulder and waved goodbye to the starter. With no rush in his step, the boy walked the 1st fairway, noticing the changes in the hues of the grass, where sections were a deeper green than others, and where clover had overtaken the turf. The greenskeeper surely must hate to see that, the boy thought. But yet there was beauty in the imperfection.

The ball was some 150 yards from the green's center, and the flag was back left, the most difficult position for hitting it close. The boy was about to step off a more exact yardage, when he stopped himself. *Why is it so important that I get it close? Why is that the goal? I'm not in competition. What does it matter?* Without an ounce of tension, the boy took a simple practice swing and then flung his approach to about twenty feet right of the pin, the swing fluid and effortless, like a step in a waltz. He could have landed it closer. He had the ability and the skill, but long shadows were beginning to form, the warm and bright late-day sun had fallen low over the tops of trees, and the boy was certain nothing, not even knocking it to six inches, could have made him feel any better than he did at that moment.

The par-3 2nd is over water. Many times, the boy had noted the looming hazard whether acknowledging it out loud or allowing its simple existence to trouble his mind. A yank to the left or a fat shot could drop the ball in the drink, and the boy could count on one hand how many times he had done either. Still, the pond had always been there, always threatened. Not this time, however. This evening it disappeared.

On the short walk to the tee at the 3rd, the boy followed the path through the wispy reeds west of the pond. He remembered once seeing a great white egret wading in the water but had forgotten until now how it sometimes flew into the tall grasses. The boy stood silent at the turn in the path, lowered his eyes, and there among the reeds in the marshy area off the pond, some five yards deep, he spotted the egret, nesting in a gathering of sticks, its long, majestic neck stretched toward the sky as if to keep watch for predators. The bird then sunk lower into its nest, pulling its body inward for comfort. All those times he had walked there. All those times he had never thought to look.

* * *

It hadn't necessarily been a hot day, but Nancy's old Taurus needed a few minutes with the air blowing and the windows down. She leaned against the trunk with the bags in her hands, waiting. Nancy had promised her friend that as long as she lived, she would keep an eye on him. Not try to change him or force him into some program or assistance he did not want. Sometimes when she would come to the 5th to deliver a meal, she would stay for a few minutes to talk—to ask if he was all right, if there was anything he needed, if he was warm enough in the chilly autumn night or cool enough in the summer, if she could bring a fresh shirt from the second-hand store. And he would thank her and decline any help, saying he was grateful for her concern and that he appreciated it, but that the food was plenty. She need not do anything else. He was okay, he would say. Not to worry, he would say. He wished not to be any kind of a burden. And when he would say this, Nancy could hear the voice of her old friend, the broadness in the way she had pronounced her vowels and how the pitch in her sentences had rolled high and low in a smooth, easy cadence. Nancy had known Jimmy's mother since grade school and had visited her every day in her final weeks. Yes, Jimmy's voice was lower, masculine, and certainly rougher now than hers had ever been, but the core tenor of his mother's voice was evident when Jimmy spoke. It was unmistakable.

Nancy reached inside the car window and touched the cloth seat with her hand. It was more comfortable now. She placed the bags on the passenger seat and climbed inside.

* * *

The late-day crew had started their work before the boy began playing and was at least a hole ahead of him. They had done this work many times before and had developed an efficient routine, gripping the oversized wooden rakes and taking opposite sides of the same bunker to work in different directions. They moved quickly, raking over their own footprints, smoothing the edges, placing the rakes in the cart, and heading to the next. It was choreography, like dancers on a stage. They had finished the traps at the 4th green and were driving toward the fairway bunker on the 5th.

"This is where he hangs out. Up there by the fence," the worker at the wheel said.

"Near the green," the other said, pointing. "He's always near that tree."

* * *

There once had been an enormous oak on the left side of the 3rd fairway. It was the hole's most strategic feature, forcing anyone who would attempt to get close to the green in two on the long par-5 to aim far to the right. It had been a beautiful tree. A lightning storm had taken it down. As the boy walked by where a sparse sapling had been planted in its place, he thought about the giant tree but could not remember when it had been lost. *Was it last summer? Two summers ago?* It had not concerned him before, hardly considering the life of the tree much at all. But now, he wished it had remained, wished it was still standing, defending the fairway, mightily protecting what it had once shaded, upright and strong.

The boy's third shot landed a yard off the right side of the green, an errant 9-iron. But instead of wedging the ball to the hole or putting, the boy picked up. He had a chance to save par on one of Old Elm's most difficult holes, but chose instead to let it be, save it for another day, for this was a different kind of round. On the path to the 4th tee, the boy spotted a yellow bird on the branch of a maple. He had heard someone say once that there were wild canaries on the golf course, and now there was one right in front of him.

* * *

Nancy pulled her car to the side of the road and sat for a moment looking out to the grassy field beyond the fence along the property line. She sighed. Looked left and right, and sighed again. There were no more late-day shadows as the sun had nearly disappeared and it wouldn't be long before evening gloominess would swallow the golf course. Behind and above her car, a streetlamp had turned on, preparing for the coming night, its light falling against the right side of Nancy's face. She had waited before and she would wait again.

* * *

The workers completed the job on the fairway trap and arrived at the 5th green, parking on the small hill on the right side.

"He's not here," one said.

"Don't see him," said the other.

Without another word, they hurried to the greenside bunker, their eyes adjusting to the lack of light to allow for one final raking.

"Who is this guy, anyway?" the first worker asked, walking to the cart after completing the job. "What's his deal? Know anything about him?"

"Nah. Just some sorry drunk," the second said. "Since I've been working here, he's always around. Everybody says so."

The worker looked down the fairway toward the tee and then across the green to the fence. "Well, he ain't around now," he said. "Don't know about you, but I wasn't really big on calling the cops on the guy."

* * *

Nancy saw the men working on the trap at the green and was

able to hear their voices, but the words were undetectable. She assumed they must have been watching for Jimmy, certain they had been told to be on the lookout. Nancy let the back of her neck fall against the seat's headrest. "An angel in disguise," she said to no one. "The stranger you do not know may be an angel in disguise."

With the sun gone and little remaining light under which to work, the two men drove away, the sputter of the cart's motor fading as they traveled.

* * *

The boy had played his way through the par-3 4th and now stood on the 5th tee in near blackness. He could see only the dark silhouettes of tall trees along the fairway. For several minutes he considered what he had come to learn about this hole, the instinctive awareness he had even after the night had swallowed it. The boy whispered into the evening air. "Jimmy?" He waited for a reply, a sound of some evidence. "Jimmy?" he asked again. But there was no answer. And in that moment, the boy's heart fell, as if he had lost something valued, something precious, as if he had misplaced an unanticipated gift. Night was falling all around him, and so the boy pulled his driver from his bag and pushed a tee in the ground. There was one more swing to make.

* * *

Nancy was outside the car, the bags in her hands, her hope of finding Jimmy had evaporated. She walked in the dark along roadside gravel and onto the grass and weeds near the big maple at the fence. Nancy heard a dog bark in the distance and the passing rumble from a car's engine, and as she placed the bags on the ground next to the trunk of the tree, she knew the coming night's sleep would offer no solace.

* * *

The boy addressed his ball, waggled his club, and stepped back. He tilted his head to the sky where the first star had appeared and watched for a moment to be sure it truly was a star and not the light of a distant plane. He rested his club against his bag, and with the laces still tied, the boy kicked off his shoes, and pulled off his socks. The grass was damp on his skin, the cool ground tickling his arches. The boy knew in what direction to aim, of course, but where the ball would land could only be determined by a combination of the sound of the strike and the muted thump of the ball landing on turf many yards away. But the boy did not concern himself with this. Where the ball would go and where it would come to rest would not matter. And so, with abandon, he gripped his club, wound up his body, and produced a powerful swing into the early night, the ball disappearing into the shadows. With his bag, shoes, and clubs behind, the boy stepped out to the fairway with naked feet and no intention of searching for the ball, no desire to find it and hit it again, no wish to finish the hole or play another. All the boy wanted was to walk in the quickening darkness with the sound of a night bird singing, calling out for someone, and to return to Old Elm on another day to watch the blackbird chase the hawk and to dream of flying high above the land like a ghost guarding the kingdom.

About the Author

David W. Berner is the author of several works of memoir and fiction. His books have won awards from the Society of Midland Authors, the Chicago Writers Association, and the Eric Hoffer Book Prize. David spent a summer writing at the Jack Kerouac House in Orlando, Florida as the honored Writer-in-Residence and was later named the Writer-in-Residence at the Ernest Hemingway Birthplace Home in Oak Park, Illinois. He is also an award-winning broadcaster and journalist, and lives outside Chicago with his wife, Leslie, and dog, Sam.

He learned the game of golf from his father on the narrow, hilly fairways of Western Pennsylvania.

**ROUNDFIRE
BOOKS**

FICTION

Put simply, we publish great stories. Whether it's literary or popular, a gentle tale or a pulsating thriller, the connecting theme in all Roundfire fiction titles is that once you pick them up you won't want to put them down.

If you have enjoyed this book, why not tell other readers by posting a review on your preferred book site.

Recent bestsellers from Roundfire are:

The Bookseller's Sonnets

Andi Rosenthal

The Bookseller's Sonnets intertwines three love stories with a tale of religious identity and mystery spanning five hundred years and three countries.

Paperback: 978-1-84694-342-3 ebook: 978-184694-626-4

Birds of the Nile

An Egyptian Adventure

N.E. David

Ex-diplomat Michael Blake wanted a quiet birding trip up the Nile – he wasn't expecting a revolution.

Paperback: 978-1-78279-158-4 ebook: 978-1-78279-157-7

The Cause

Roderick Vincent

The second American Revolution will be a fire lit from an internal spark.

Paperback: 978-1-78279-763-0 ebook: 978-1-78279-762-3

Blood Profit$

The Lithium Conspiracy

J. Victor Tomaszek, James N. Patrick, Sr.

The blood of the many for the profits of the few… *Blood Profit$* will take you into the cigar-smoke-filled room where American policy and laws are really made.

Paperback: 978-1-78279-483-7 ebook: 978-1-78279-277-2

The Burden
A Family Saga
N.E. David
Frank will do anything to keep his mother and father apart. But
he's carrying baggage – and it might just weigh him down …
Paperback: 978-1-78279-936-8 ebook: 978-1-78279-937-5

Don't Drink and Fly
The Story of Bernice O'Hanlon: Part One
Cathie Devitt
Bernice is a witch living in Glasgow. She loses her way in her
life and wanders off the beaten track looking for the garden of
enlightenment.
Paperback: 978-1-78279-016-7 ebook: 978-1-78279-015-0

Gag
Melissa Unger
One rainy afternoon in a Brooklyn diner, Peter Howland punctures
an egg with his fork. Repulsed, Peter pushes the plate away and
never eats again.
Paperback: 978-1-78279-564-3 ebook: 978-1-78279-563-6

The Master Yeshua
The Undiscovered Gospel of Joseph
Joyce Luck
Jesus is not who you think he is. The year is 75 CE. Joseph ben Jude
is frail and ailing, but he has a prophecy to fulfil …
Paperback: 978-1-78279-974-0 ebook: 978-1-78279-975-7

On the Far Side, There's a Boy
Paula Coston
Martine Haslett, a thirty-something 1980s woman, plays hard on
the fringes of the London drag club scene until one night which
prompts her to sign up to a charity. She writes to a young Sri
Lankan boy, with consequences far and long.
Paperback: 978-1-78279-574-2 ebook: 978-1-78279-573-5

Tuareg
Alberto Vazquez-Figueroa
With over 5 million copies sold worldwide, *Tuareg* is a classic
adventure story from best-selling author Alberto Vazquez-
Figueroa, about honour, revenge and a clash of cultures.
Paperback: 978-1-84694-192-4

Readers of ebooks can buy or view any of these bestsellers by
clicking on the live link in the title. Most titles are published in
paperback and as an ebook. Paperbacks are available in traditional
bookshops. Both print and ebook formats are available online.

Find more titles and sign up to our readers' newsletter at
http://www.johnhuntpublishing.com/fiction

Follow us on Facebook at https://www.facebook.com/JHPfiction
and Twitter at https://twitter.com/JHPFiction